THE DUKE'S DOVE

Twelve Days of Christmas - Book 2

LAUREN SMITH

ISBN: 978-1-952063-04-6 (e-book edition)

ISBN: 978-1-952063-05-3 (print edition)

ON THE SECOND DAY OF
CHRISTMAS MY TRUE LOVE
GAVE TO ME...

E *ngland—Christmas Eve 1821*

"IT'S A DAMN COLD NIGHT, EH, NATHAN?"

Nathan Powell, the Duke of Hastings, glanced in irritation at his younger brother, Lewis, who was just visible in the light from the coach lantern. The flame rippled and sputtered as the lantern rocked slightly with the moving conveyance. It was a poor night to be out on the road and traveling. Nathan's mood was often dark of late, but now it was bleaker than ever. When they'd set out from his estate, only a few miles away, the skies were already heavy with winter storm clouds. It would be his luck to be snowed in for Christmas at someone else's home.

Christmas was a holiday he very much despised. It was a season of love, of joy, of hope. The three things he no longer had. But that was to be expected when he'd had his heart broken eight years ago.

"Nathan, you didn't have to come tonight." Lewis's usually teasing tone softened. "I know how you feel about this time of year. Perhaps you could try to enjoy it, just this once?" Lewis was only twenty-five, three years younger than Nathan, and he still had the fresh hope that youth carried when it came to the holidays.

Nathan knew his brother didn't mean to sound pitying, yet he did, and it set his teeth on edge. As a duke, it was not his place to be pitied by anyone. His father had taught him that very well indeed. A duke was a man of power, and his very title demanded respect, even from his own family.

"I promised Sir Giles I would make an appearance," Nathan grumbled.

Giles Pemberton had been a dear friend of his mother and father, more so to his mother than the late duke—that man had had few true friends. His sour demeanor and rigid control had left much to be desired when it came to forming lasting relationships with anyone, including his own wife and children.

"Yes, well, I'm sure Sir Giles will be glad you

came. I certainly am. It wouldn't do at all to show up without you to something so grand as this." Lewis's mood was already brightening again as he seemed to be thinking ahead to the grand party that awaited them.

It had taken quite a bit of convincing from Lewis to make the party seem worthwhile for Nathan. He kept to himself these days, focusing on the tenant farms and his time spent in London while he served in the House of Lords. All else had lost meaning to him in the last several years. Life itself had withered away, each moment lacking a purpose, a reason to continue.

I've become an empty shell.

Lewis started speaking again, the entire conversation nearly one-sided—not that Nathan minded. He wasn't even paying attention to what his brother was saying. Lewis was an easygoing sort and always had something to say, but Nathan no longer had the heart to participate. As children, they had been close, almost inseparable. When Nathan's dreams for the future had been cut to pieces, his relationship with his brother, his mother—his relationships with everyone—had withered like a vine in winter. Nathan gazed out the coach window, lost in thoughts as his eyes roved over the miles of snow-covered land.

Lewis is a lucky devil. He envied Lewis's freedom.

As the head of his family, Nathan had few choices

he could make freely. Even after obeying all the rules, he'd lost so much. *Far too much.* He buried the bittersweet memories deep in his splintered heart, welcoming the ache in his chest. It was a pain he deserved because he had caused it.

"How much farther?" he growled.

"He speaks at last," Lewis said with a laugh. "Any minute now." His brother peered through the small coach window. "I believe I see the lights from the house."

They emerged from a line of evergreens to the welcoming sight of Pemberton Hall, the home of Sir Giles and his family. The lights from the house illuminated the white snow, casting a gold glow. A few coaches ahead of them were lined up before the grand doorway into the Palladian-style manor house.

The hall itself was an expanse of tan stone nestled among trees that were laced with fresh snow. The windows on the ground floor were illuminated with candles, and Nathan could see the dancing couples as his coach stopped before the doors.

"We're here," Lewis announced with a grin. For a brief moment his eyes locked with Nathan's, and Nathan didn't miss the hint of pain in Lewis's eyes. "I hope we're in time for the festivities." The words sounded a little forced, as though he feared he wouldn't enjoy the evening if Nathan did not. That bothered Nathan greatly. Lewis was entitled to live his own life, make his own fortune, and choose his own fate. He didn't deserve to suffer alongside Nathan.

"It's a ball. You'll have hours to seduce the young ladies." Nathan's lips formed a thin smile as he attempted to tease his brother. It had been so long that he'd almost forgotten how. "I'm sure there's plenty of mistletoe to aid you in your nefarious mission."

"Seduction is nefarious? Gracious, I am quite a devil then," Lewis quipped. "What about you, brother? Finally going to settle upon a duchess now that . . ." He didn't finish, but Nathan knew what words he'd nearly said.

Now that you're free of Father's control.

"Heavens, no. I plan to die without an heir so that you might inherit all the trouble." Nathan did actually smile more naturally this time as he saw Lewis's mock look of horror.

"Never say so, Nathan. You know I'd make a terrible duke. Sitting all day in the House of Lords, listening to men bicker and gripe. And apparently more than a few of those lords snore . . ." His little brother shuddered. "Yes, we must find a young lady for you tonight, and you shall beget an heir at once, if only to spare your beloved brother from becoming a duke."

"You may be the only man in England who'd refuse a dukedom."

"And rightly so. What a mess I'd make of things," Lewis said quite honestly. "Now, let's see. Sir Giles sent me a list of who was invited to the ball. Shall I run down the names for you?"

Since Nathan had no intention of actually seeking out a lady to marry, he found no harm in letting his brother play the matchmaker while they waited for a footman to assist them.

"Very well, who is on this list of yours?"

"There is an Italian countess recently widowed— Rafaela Sabatini. Rumored to be quite a beauty, but likely has a temper. You know how those Italians can be."

"I think the term you're searching for is *passionate*, Lewis. Italians are passionate."

"Right, passionate." Lewis's blue eyes glowed with mischief. "And then there's Emma Christie, the daughter of Viscount Fordham. I hear she's quite adept at cards. Never play against her if you value your coin."

"Lewis," Nathan said with a chuckle. "I'm sensing that the ladies who caught your attention all seem to have a bit of a vice."

"Well, vice is more interesting, isn't it? Would you really want to meet a lady who has nothing interesting about her? A girl who paints silly watercolors or gossips over tea? Christ, no. A man needs a woman who has the same desire for a colorful and interesting life as he does." Lewis declared this with such an air of ancient wisdom about him that Nathan decided Lewis had to be teasing him.

"Very well, what of the boring chits? Regale me with tales of them," Nathan demanded and bit his lip to hide a smile.

"Boring chits . . ." Lewis tapped his chin. "There's always one or two Poncenbys running about. Pepper, I believe, is still unwed."

"Let us pass by Pepper. I cannot stand that dandy she calls a brother."

"Very well, no Poncenbys. Well, the Russells might be there."

"I thought you said you were telling me about boring chits. Lysandra Russell is rumored to be a rather interesting eccentric, and I have no interest in tangling with her wild brothers, no matter how fascinating the lady might be."

Only then did Nathan see a gleam of cleverness in Lewis's eyes that told him he'd played right into his brother's plans.

"Well, there is one more family worth mentioning. John Swann is in attendance tonight, along with his family." Lewis rubbed his palms over his thighs in eagerness. "A multitude of opportunities there."

"The Swanns are coming? Why didn't you

mention this from the very start? You know very well I wouldn't have come. I . . ." Nathan's words died upon his lips. For a second, he couldn't think, couldn't breathe. Would *she* be here tonight? The woman he'd loved and lost nearly a decade ago?

"So I've been told. All seven of Swann's daughters were invited." Lewis cast a curious glance at Nathan. "Didn't you almost propose to one of them? Thea, wasn't it?"

"You know damned well I planned to marry her before Father prevented it!" Nathan nearly snarled. His fury had returned.

"That's right . . . Well, I was a young lad when you did that. I was more focused on putting frogs in the cook's apron pockets than I was listening to you about your romantic affairs. I certainly avoided Father whenever I could," Lewis reminded him gently, but it didn't erase the blinding pain that filled Nathan's chest.

Theodosia Swann. *My Thea.* Even after all these years, Nathan's heart still claimed her as its own. He'd only ever loved one woman, only ever wanted one woman. And despite having a duty to produce an heir, he could not envision a life with anyone else, not after having loved and lost Thea. He must live in this hell of his own making because he deserved it— because he'd broken her heart along with his own. She would be six and twenty years old by now, likely married to some man. She would have a handful of children—children Nathan would have given anything to have fathered.

"Surely most of the Swann sisters are married by now," Lewis mused. "There might still be one or two young enough to . . ." But Nathan ignored whatever Lewis said next, letting his thoughts run away with him, far back into the past.

E ight years ago

"FATHER?" NATHAN STEPPED INTO HIS FATHER'S study. The duke was seated at his desk, his head bent as he looked over a stack of papers.

"What is it?" his father barked at him.

"I . . . uh . . . sir, I wish to have an audience with you. It is of the utmost importance." He glanced back toward the door, where his mother stood just outside. She nodded in encouragement. She had convinced him that now was the time to seek his father's permission to marry. His mother approved of the match, of course. Who would not adore Thea Swann?

His mother waved a hand at him, and then she quietly closed the study door to give Nathan privacy with his father.

"What could be so bloody important? I have to review these letters by the end of the day and have my answers composed at once, so out with it, boy," Hastings snapped.

Nathan had practiced this speech a thousand times. He desperately wanted to tell his father all the things that lay in his heart, yet he feared what would happen when he did so. His father was a cold man, a man who didn't believe love or passion should exist in a marriage. He believed in land, money, and powerful connections. Thea's family offered none of that. They were but landed gentry from the country. Yet anyone who had met Thea would know that she would make a perfect duchess.

"I wish to propose to Miss Swann today. I've already spoken to her father about it, and he has given his consent."

The duke raised his head, this time his full attention focused on Nathan.

"You are planning to do what?" The iron edge to his tone warned Nathan that this was not pleasing news to his father.

"I . . . wish to marry Miss Swann."

"No." The reply was so quick that for a second Nathan thought he'd merely imagined it.

"Father—"

"No." His eyes were frosted with quiet rage as he gazed at Nathan. "A pretty face is not important. You must marry wisely. I will choose your bride for you. And you will not marry, not yet. You shall wait until you are at least five and twenty before you select a bride."

"But—"

"That is my final word. You will not disobey me."

Nathan's own anger rose. "I will not disobey you? Pray, tell me, Father, what can you do to stop me? I am twenty years old, well within my rights to marry if I choose, and the lady's father has consented." He had made his choice. He would not let his father stop him from marrying Thea.

"What can I do?" His father didn't even stand to face him. His cruel lips twisted in a terrifying smile. "I can purchase the debts Mr. Swann owes his creditors—and I can take his whole world away from him and his brood of useless daughters. When he is penniless and starving and his daughters are whoring themselves, you'll be the one to blame."

Nathan acted without a second thought and lunged across the desk, fist swinging, and he struck his father. The man grunted and fell out of his chair to the floor. He touched his mouth, blood coating his lip, but he curled that lip in a sneer as he gazed up at Nathan.

"Never speak of Thea or her family that way again," Nathan warned. Cold fury to rival his father's layered every word.

"Be careful, boy. I'll let this pass today, but if you dare breathe that chit's name again or speak against me, I will destroy her and her family without a second thought."

Nathan didn't doubt his father's threats. He'd never imagined that his father wouldn't approve of Thea. The Swanns were a good family. They were not an embarrassment, and they had no scandal attached to their name. They simply weren't of the peerage. Nathan hadn't fathomed that would be a crime. Yet clearly it was to his father—enough to ruin his life and Thea's if he didn't end his understanding with her.

Nathan straightened his waistcoat and stepped outside of his father's study, his head a little fuzzy and his ears ringing as though he had been the one to take the blow and not his father.

"Nathan? What did he say?" His mother had been hovering nearby, and she came straight to him.

"I cannot have her, Mother," Nathan whispered, the words slicing his throat. "He will not let me marry Thea."

"Oh . . . oh, my poor boy." His mother put an arm around his shoulders as his world crumbled around him.

When his gaze met hers, he saw her sorrow, her pain. She understood better than anyone what having a life destroyed meant. Marrying the Duke of Hastings had stolen her away from the man she'd truly loved and wished to marry, but she'd been trying to help her own family out of difficulties. She too had burdens to bear when it came to the cruelty of her husband. He did not raise a hand to her, but his words and his moods were black enough to wound as deeply.

"He . . . he said he would ruin Mr. Swann if I married Thea against his wishes. I am not even to speak her name . . ." For the past two years, Nathan had felt like a man, not a boy, yet in the last few minutes his father had reduced him to a frightened child. All he could think of was Thea and what would happen to her if he did not obey.

"You must go see her one last time. Tell her the truth. She deserves to hear it from you. Then you must let her go. Someone new will love her, marry her and give her all that you cannot. While your own heart breaks, you will take comfort in knowing she is safe and happy, even though she is not with you." His mother's words choked slightly as her own pain from the past bled into her speech. Her dark hair, streaked now with hints of silver, and the blue eyes that held such love for him and Lewis now clouded with tears.

"Mother—"

"You will always know that I understand what it means to lose the one you love. I am here for you, my boy. Always." She'd dried her eyes, and he'd regained some of his composure, enough to walk her back to her own private withdrawing room, where she could have some time to grieve for her own past.

He squared his shoulders and walked toward the front door. A young groom met him at the door, and he called for his horse to be readied. The Swann manor house was not far, only a quarter of an hour on horseback.

During the ride toward Thea's home, his head was strangely empty of thought and his heart devoid of emotion. It was as though some part of him had already died or simply faded away, knowing that he'd lost her.

Nathan slid off his horse when he reached the front door of the Swann home. A groom collected his reins, and a footman took his hat and gloves.

"I'm here to see Miss Swann," he informed the butler.

"Of course, my lord." The butler bowed and went to find Thea.

The Swann home, while not as grand as his own, was warm and comforting, an air of country-house comfort filling every room. The wildflowers painted upon the walls and the warm walnut wood paneling of the rooms made every day feel like spring, even in the midst of the harshest winters. This house, in many ways, had been more a home to Nathan than Hastings Hall.

"My lord, she is in the orchard, if you wish to join her."

"Thank you." He nodded at the butler and walked through the house, knowing full well the way to the orchard.

He stepped out onto the back terrace, his heart swelling with a sudden desperate longing as he saw the avenue of green grass lined with blossoming cherry trees. The pink-and-white blooms bedecked every branch of every tree as far as his eye could see. Nathan descended the stone steps and set foot on the soft emerald-green grass. A gentle hush always filled the Swann gardens, as though one had simply slipped into the most wonderful dream just before dawn was about to break. Not a bird trilled too loudly, not a rose grew too many thorns. It was a paradise unlike anything he'd ever known. He moved down the avenue of the pink blur of cherry trees. As their branches quivered and wavered in the slight breeze, they sounded like a dozen women whispering softly behind their bright-pink fans.

What secrets can the trees read upon my face? Will they know I've come to break their mistress's heart?

At the end of the lane, beneath the dappled shade of a stout tree, was Thea, a book in her hands.

He wanted to run, to call out her name, to erase the fight with his father, but that could never be undone, unless he was willing to hurt her and her family.

Stopping just short of a dozen feet from her, Nathan's breath failed him when he first attempted to call out her name.

"Thea . . ." It was barely above a whisper, yet the breeze carried the sound to her.

She looked up, her auburn hair glowing like summer gold as her face lit with the smile that had captured his heart when he'd been only fourteen.

I have loved you, my Thea, more than you can ever know.

The words were only spoken within himself. They would have cut him to ribbons if he had tried to form them aloud.

"Nathan!" She leapt to her feet and tossed the book gently onto the grass. Her rose-colored gown was so rich a color, matching the blush of life within her cheeks, that it made his heart stutter in its beats.

"Thea, wait—" He tried to raise his hands as she threw herself against him, covering his face with kisses as she often did. But this time he couldn't return them.

He captured her wrists gently and slowly pushed her away from him.

"Nathan, what's wrong?" she asked. The glow of

her natural joy diminished as she studied his face more clearly.

"I . . . spoke with my father." And that was how he began to tell the woman he loved more than his own life that he could not give her what they had both dreamt of for years.

"He won't let us marry?" she asked faintly as she pulled her wrists free of his hands. He let her go, feeling the chasm deepen between them.

"I told him I would marry you without his permission, but he threatened your father, your whole family. He said your sisters would be out upon the streets—" He stopped, unable to speak the full horror of what his father had warned would befall them. "Thea, please look at me," he begged.

She raised her eyes to his, and he saw his entire universe collapse in her eyes, like the death of some distant star that had always guided him home. Now that star was gone, and he was cast adrift, lost forever in a sea of night.

"But I love you . . . ," she replied, as though those words held the answer to any challenge they would ever face together.

"Would you condemn your family to suffer?" Nathan asked quietly. "Would you watch your father become a broken man? Would you want to lose your home and see your mother and sisters starve? I cannot bear that burden. I love you too much. Do you understand?" Where he found the strength to say this he would never know.

"I understand." Her voice was very small, like a child who had suddenly learned that she must grow up. Nathan wished then that he could have lied to her, that he could have held her in his arms and told her all would be well, that their lives weren't on separate paths that would tear them apart forever.

He reached for her, catching her in his arms when she tried to escape him. She struggled against him before her body surrendered and buried her face against his chest, soaking his waistcoat with her tears. Nathan's head tilted upward, and he stared through the canopy of brilliant pink-and-white blossoms toward the unforgiving sky far above. A shuddering sigh escaped him as he held her in his arms, his heart beating for what felt like the first time in years, She had always owned his heart. It beat only for her. That would never change.

"Thea, I will love you until the last star in the sky perishes—and perhaps even beyond." He swallowed thickly. "You will promise me something." He raised her chin with one hand so that she met his eyes. "Promise me that you will live a full life. Find a man who will love and adore you and have a passel of children so that someday . . . I will hear of your joy and it will give me some small measure of peace."

"Nathan . . ." Her greenish-gray eyes filled with

tears, and the sight of her pain in that moment would haunt him until he drew his last breath.

"Swear to me," he demanded.

She nodded.

"I need to hear the words from your lips." He cupped her face.

"I swear it." Her voice was firm, but her sorrow and grief were living things, morphing into darkening shadows in her eyes, betraying her strength.

He wanted to kiss her, but if he did, he would never find his own strength to let go.

Nathan released her, stepped back, and with one last look full of regret, he walked away. The sound of her sobbing his name dug black holes in his heart that would never heal.

*C*hristmas Eve 1821

THE PAST WAS NOW A PAINFUL THING, A CREATURE that no one wanted to see drawn into the light. Yet Nathan was going to face his past tonight in Sir Giles's ballroom. He cast a glance at his brother. Lewis, as the spare to the heir, had escaped much of their father's vitriol and had managed to find joy in life, where Nathan and their mother had failed. He seemed completely unperturbed by Nathan's sudden, stony silence.

Lewis was still talking, unaware that Nathan had

slipped back into his memories a moment ago and was only just now listening to Lewis's excited chatter.

"Too many of the Swann ladies are still unwed. Which means I shall have to tread carefully. Wouldn't want Mr. Swann catching me compromising one of his daughters. He'd have my head or my proposal. Neither situation appeals to me." Lewis snickered.

Nathan shook his head. Someday Lewis would be trapped either in a marriage or a duel.

A young, ruddy-faced footman rushed out to meet them and opened the door. "Welcome, Your Grace, my lord. We're so sorry about the delay. The other carriages were stuck in the snow, and it took us a minute to move them." He bowed to Lewis and Nathan.

Nathan offered a weary smile to the lad. He was probably the only man in England who wasn't fond of having a title—or at least he wasn't fond of the responsibilities and expectations that came with it. The only benefit was it meant his father was dead. There had been no love lost between the late Duke of Hastings and his two sons, even before their father had prevented Nathan from proposing to Thea.

The "Old Curmudgeon," as Lewis often called him, had been bad-tempered, even on his best days. There was no satisfying him, no pleasing him. It was only after the man had died unexpectedly that Nathan had realized he'd given up everything he'd loved, when he could have asked Thea to wait. But then, at twenty years old, Nathan hadn't been able to see eight years into the future and know his father would be gone. All he'd known was that his father would likely have tried to live forever just to spite Nathan. And now it was too late. Thea was no doubt married. She would have kept her word as she'd promised that awful day.

Fresh pain pricked his heart as he knew he would face her for the first time since they'd last seen each other eight years ago. Despite the general closeness of upper-class English society, he'd kept himself far away from any social circles that would have brought her into his view or even into conversation.

Yes, he'd demanded that she agree to move on, but that didn't mean he wanted to be forced to face that painful reality again and again. He'd accepted that he was a coward long ago. So he'd become a recluse, hiding away at his estate in the country or traveling north to see to his land holdings in Scotland. His plan had worked. He'd heard not one word about Thea or any of the Swanns, and for that he'd been grateful—until tonight.

"You all right, brother?" Lewis asked as they both stood facing the front door of Sir Giles's home.

"No, no, I'm afraid I'm not," he muttered.

Lewis quirked a questioning brow. "Perhaps Thea won't be here tonight."

"I fear luck is never with a man like me." She would most certainly be here, and he would be forced to watch her dance around the ballroom with a dashing man and hear whispers of her beautiful children and wonderful life, every bit of which she deserved.

His little brother clapped a gloved hand on his shoulder. "We shan't stay long, then. A few dances and we can make our apologies and slip away."

"No, I don't wish to deprive you of tonight's merriment. I will endure." Nathan tried to sound teasing, but from the look of pity on Lewis's face, he knew he'd failed miserably.

They ascended the steps to the black-painted oak doors of Pemberton Hall, tramping through the thick snow that layered the stone stairs, where the butler waited to take their greatcoats. Lewis, only a few steps ahead of Nathan, turned to flash him a smile and a wink before ducking into the grand ballroom, where he quickly vanished into the crowd.

Nathan scowled. He despised these social gatherings. Everyone attempted to throw their daughters under his feet, as though expecting him to propose marriage the second he tripped over them. More than once he'd narrowly avoided being trapped alone in a room with a young woman.

Once in that very scenario, he'd realized he was about to be "discovered" alone with a trembling young woman who clearly was terrified to be alone with a man. He'd made a hasty apology and run to the nearest window, which thankfully had been partially opened. Just as the girl's father's boots in the hall heralded Nathan's doom, Nathan had leapt clear through into a patch of thick hedges. He'd then ducked down and crawled upon his belly through the flower beds along the base of the house, careful to avoid detection by the father, who'd expected to find his daughter in the arms of a duke. During his crawling escape, Nathan had nearly choked in fear as he'd come face to face with a pair of boots. When he'd lifted his head, he'd been relieved to see a gardener, not the girl's father, staring down at him.

"Your Grace?" the man had asked.

"Sorry, my good man. Just thought I'd take a turn about the gardens. Could you kindly have a groom bring my horse around?"

The gardener had chuckled. "Of course, Your Grace. You wouldn't be the first man crawling to freedom, I'll tell you that much." The old man had walked off chuckling.

The memory of that particularly fine spring day of him riding away at a breakneck pace from that manor house, his waistcoat ruined with soil, caused him almost to smile. *Almost.* Thea would have laughed at him. She— He stopped that thought before it could continue.

The sudden prospect of possibly seeing Thea again had him on edge with a mix of anticipation and dire dread, the combination of which was tossing his insides about as though he were on a ship in the midst of a vast and mighty storm. He ran his hand over his jaw and tried to still his nerves. Was she here? His hands were shaking as he tried in vain to steady himself. Would he see her standing there with the glow of love in her eyes for another man? If he did, could he bear it? Even if he couldn't, he had to try—he had to do it for her. She couldn't see him agonized like that; she didn't deserve it. With a deep breath, Nathan stepped into Sir Giles's ballroom.

The elegant golden-floored ballroom teemed with local gentry and many familiar faces from London. Sir Giles was a rare sort of man who could call the lowest gentlemen up to dukes his friends and get them all to pleasantly mingle without incident. Candles cast flickering shadows along the walls of those who stood talking and laughing. Light and laughter filled the room. A string quartet played lively tunes, filling the room with the delightful sounds. It would have been a magical night if it weren't for the stabbing pain of his broken heart.

He closed his eyes only briefly, willing himself with all his heart to pretend that this night was a night from eight years ago, a night in the past where he was still young, still hopeful. When he opened his eyes again, the world seemed to glow just a bit brighter, the laughter rang a bit louder, and his heart was a bit less . . . broken. Yes, he could hold this illusion together for a few hours, for his brother's sake.

Along the back of the narrow end of the ballroom a long table was adorned with a white cloth. Food and freshly poured glasses of champagne and ratafia on top of the table were ready for the guests. Quite a few of the younger men lingered around a punch bowl that Nathan suspected contained far too many spirits, judging by the grins on their eager faces. That was bound to be trouble later. His lips twitched as he saw Lewis among the young men, talking and laughing, always at the center of trouble.

He smoothed his hands over his white linen shirt and tugged on the edges of his black superfine coat. Even though there was not a single wrinkle in his clothing, he felt . . . unsettled and unprepared for whatever was to come.

Damned balls. He hated formal attire, but the black breeches and stockings were an unfortunate requirement. He'd even allowed his valet to talk him into the Trone d'Amour style of folds for his cravat tonight. A fleet-footed thought darted through his mind as he studied the ladies nearest him, searching for the one woman who mattered. Would Thea still think him handsome? Would she still be in awe of him as she had been so long ago? Or would that husband he'd beseeched her to find now be the sole focus of her heart? Of course he would. His and Thea's love had been a first love—no less strong, no less important, but it was untried, untested by the might of destiny. She would look upon him with a fondness for that dim, golden, glowing memory of what they'd once shared. But it would pain her no longer, of that he must be certain. Thea loved too greatly to not give the man she married her full heart.

I will be but a phantom of her youth in her mind, nothing more, and I must be content.

He focused on the women around him and studied the numerous faces surrounded by ringlets or half-hidden by fluttering fans. Attracted by any flicker of feminine movement, he sought Thea's likeness in each face, yet he didn't see her. His heart dropped, and his forced smile faltered. Maybe she wasn't here.

Relief warred with disappointment. He pushed his way deeper into the ballroom, noticing an alcove he hadn't seen from his former position. He took refuge there, hoping to get a better glimpse of the women in the room. Leaning against the marble column nearest him, he crossed his arms over his chest and stayed within the shadows provided by the alcove as he continued to survey the room.

Evergreen strands circled the columns at the edges of the room, and boughs of mistletoe had been hung with care above many of the windows where couples might linger and steal a kiss when no one was watching. Gentlemen escorted women who wore their best evening gowns as they moved about. Each time a man lowered his head to whisper to his female companion and Nathan saw an answering smile, flashes of heartbreak and envy rippled through him.

The press of so many bodies and the general noise of the social chatter all around him was smothering. He couldn't stay here much longer. Deciding to seek out fresh air, even if it was freezing, he straightened from his leaning position and searched for the best way to sneak out into the terraced gardens outside.

The dancers nearest him moved in and out of view as they twirled. When a large group of couples passed by, they revealed a glowing presence just beyond. He stood there, struck still as he saw Theodosia Swann for the first time in eight years. She was just as beautiful as before—even more so. His breath froze in his lungs as he drank in the sight of her.

She wore a deep-emerald satin gown, with a gold netting overskirt that glittered as she moved. Her hair was pulled back from her face, with matching green ribbons threaded among her silken locks. Easily the most beautiful woman in the ballroom tonight, she had become the woman he'd always known she would be, the woman who by rights should have been his.

His mouth dried, and he struggled to swallow past the lump in his throat. His body was rooted to the spot as he stood stiff and taut with indecision. Should he go to her? What would she want him to do? Would she be happy to see him? Would she smile at him and recall fond memories of their youthful love, or would she wish to avoid him? Had she dreamt of him every night as he did her, or would her husband now rightfully occupy the realm of her dreams?

Thea stood out in the midst of her six younger sisters like the North Star in the winter skies, shimmering, glittering, all alone in the dark expanse of the inky universe. Yet she was none the weaker for it. She was brighter, more enchanting.

Thea. My Thea.

He was enraptured by her as he watched her whisper something to one of her sisters. Her auburn hair caught the light of the candles nearest her, a beacon shining for him. Her greenish-gray eyes, jade pools frosted with silver, glanced about the room; she was unaware of the steady heat of his own gaze.

Nathan sucked in a harsh breath as his body stirred to life with a level of arousal he'd thought he'd never feel again. Eight years had wrought great changes in her. In them both. The lithe-bodied girl of seventeen he'd swept across ballrooms in her first Season was gone. In her place was a woman infinitely more alluring, with luscious curves his hands itched to touch and pale-pink lips he longed to explore with his own. Were they as soft as he remembered?

She smoothed her hands over her dark-green gown and tugged at the puffed sleeves trimmed with lace. Her full breasts were accented by a square-cut neckline and a bodice embroidered with holly leaves. Like a ghost of a Christmas long forgotten, she was haunting and exquisite.

When she shifted, he caught a glimpse of the shape of her legs as the silk, drawn up in festoons with more holly leaves, rustled and clung to her. Most men preferred younger women, girls barely out of their first Season, but Nathan couldn't think of anything more lovely, more sensual, than a full-grown woman who had a body worth holding, worth making love to endlessly into the night.

Her gaze swept the room, and his gut clenched a second before her eyes hit him with the force of a physical blow. He swallowed hard as he watched as her cheeks turned from blooming roses to ash. The look on her face robbed him of breath. Sadness etched into her features, and he hated seeing it, seeing her so wounded. She looked as destroyed on the outside at seeing him as he had been on the inside on the day he'd broken both their hearts.

His heart cried out for her. *Things are different now. I'm not the fool I once was, and I'm not under my father's control. But I am too late, aren't I?*

Thea gave up herding her six younger sisters deeper into the ballroom. It was a bit like herding six wild geese. They seemed content to gossip and twitter like peahens about the latest fashions, who was in love with whom, and which couples had secret understandings. At this last part, Thea rolled her eyes. Wasn't the point of a secret understanding to actually be a secret? When she had been younger, she'd had an understanding once, very secret, up until the day she'd expected a proposal . . . a proposal that never came.

"Thea? By God's teeth! It has been positively ages!" A familiar voice made her halt in the path of chasing after her sisters, who were bustling toward the refreshment table. She turned to see a tall, handsome man moving toward her. For a moment she couldn't breathe, but as her eyes took in the figure approaching, she exhaled in relief.

It wasn't Nathan. It was his younger brother, Lewis.

"Oh, heavens, Lewis, it's you." She laughed a little, and he didn't seem to notice the edge to the sound.

"Hello, Thea," Lewis said more softly as he reached her and held out his hands. She clasped them, smiling. Lewis had grown up in the last three years since she'd crossed paths with him at Gunter's, where she'd been out with a few companions eating flavored ices. He looked very much like Nathan, only without the world-weary weight upon his brow of the dukedom.

"Lewis, how is your mother?"

"Well enough. Lonely, perhaps. She would love it very much if you came to call."

For a moment she couldn't respond as her throat tightened. She could see herself riding her horse down the lane toward the ancestral home of the Powells. She could see in her mind's eye the towering oak trees that lined the road, their branches arching over to create a wooded passage as though to a magical realm.

How many nights had she closed her eyes and traveled that path, over and over, again and again, reaching the door to the home she'd wanted to share with the only man who'd ever held her heart? But the dream always ended just as her hands touched the door, and the golden dream faded into a crushing darkness that left her shaking, sobs tearing from her throat.

"Say you will come and visit her, Thea, please." Lewis's plea seemed to hold a note of such seriousness that she didn't feel comfortable denying him.

"I suppose I could come . . . only if . . ." She bit her lip before continuing. "Only if I knew that I would not intrude upon your brother."

At this, Lewis's gaze sharpened. "You wouldn't be intruding—you know that, Thea. He would be glad to see you."

Determined to avoid the subject that would inevitably wound her, she asked instead, "How are you? I know that the loss of your father must not have been easy."

The young man smiled grimly. "I wish I could be a good son and say I am grieving his loss. But I am not a good son. His death was freeing for all of us, especially Nathan."

"Oh . . ." She didn't know what to say.

"Thea . . . he is here tonight. I know you likely don't wish to see him, but . . . would you see him at least once tonight? One dance? It is Christmas, after all."

She didn't speak. Her heart was pounding a wild rhythm. Nathan was here? He never came to social functions, not since that awful day in the orchards of her family home.

"One dance is all I ask of you," Lewis begged. "One dance for him to remember."

She found herself nodding, her tongue too tied to form words.

"Thank you. I shall endeavor to go find him. He's so damned clever at hiding away at these sorts of things." Lewis bowed over her hand and went in search of his brother.

But there was no need. As always, fate seemed to draw them together. Several couples moved past her, then split apart, revealing him standing just across the room.

"Nathan!" she gasped. She blinked rapidly, trying to dispel the dream that had descended over her vision.

Nathan, now the Duke of Hastings. She'd forgotten how tall he was, standing several inches above the men nearest him. His dark hair was tousled and longer than she remembered, curling at the edges of his collar. His eyes, such a warm hazel, had always heated her body like a wildfire whenever he looked her way. They were fixed on her now, and in a blinding rush, the past came crashing back, inescapable, inevitable.

4

T welve years ago

FOURTEEN-YEAR-OLD THEA TIED UP HER SKIRTS using a bit of twine to fashion a set of loose trousers about her legs. She stripped out of her stockings and boots, setting them upon the bank of the stream. Then she retrieved her fishing pole and the small tin of worms before she waded barefoot into the shallows. The cold water was crisp against her skin and soft as silk as it rushed past her and over the smooth riverbed stones beneath her feet. Tiny minnows darted around her, tickling her as their slick fins brushed against her ankles.

The noonday sun beat down in warm rays against her bare arms, face, and neck, the feeling quite wonderful. There was nothing better than fishing on a clear summer day. She captured a worm from her small tin, and it wriggled while she set it upon the hook before she tossed her fishing line out in the rushing water, farther away where the larger fish would be.

Thea wasn't sure how long she'd stood there, immersing herself in the sound of the water and the feel of the breeze against her skin, before noticing she wasn't alone.

A young man astride a pretty roan mare was on the opposite side of the stream. He slowly slid out of the saddle and walked his horse to the water's edge, where the horse bent its head to drink. For a moment they simply stared at each other. He looked to be only a year or perhaps two older than her, enough that he was already looking the part of a young gentleman. His dark hair and bewitching eyes fit the attractive, handsome features of his face.

"Hello there. I didn't mean to startle you," he said with a warm smile.

"Hello," Thea replied, uncertain of what to do. She was the eldest of her sisters, but she was still too young to be out in society, conversing with a gentleman.

"Have you had any luck?" he asked.

"Luck?" she asked, a bit dumbstruck as he began to walk his horse across the shallow stream toward her.

"Yes," he chuckled. "With the fish," he clarified. "I've been to a spot farther upstream, but I have the damnedest bad luck there." He walked his horse over to the nearest group of trees behind them and tied the reins, then returned to stand at the shore.

"Do you mind if I join you?" he asked as he stripped off his boots and stockings.

"No," Thea finally managed to say. "I don't mind." She watched him wade into the water, fascinated by him. He was taller than her, by perhaps a head, and his shoulders were broad. It made something inside her go very still, yet there was a fluttering, too, an excited feeling as if a hummingbird had managed to find a way inside her chest.

"My name is Nathan Powell." He held out a hand to her to shake it, which all together something only a young man would do with other boys. Strangely the casual greeting put her more at ease than if he'd tried to kiss her hand. She certainly wouldn't have known how to react to that.

"I'm Thea Swann." She shook his hand and tried to still the increased flutterings of that invisible bird inside her.

"Do you like to fish?" he asked when she offered him her pole. He gave a few experimental tugs on it to see if moving the lure in the water might attract a fish.

"I do. Do you?" she asked.

He chuckled. "I do. My father says it's not an elegant sport for a gentleman, but I don't care. It's . . . peaceful." He said this with such an adult seriousness that it almost made her laugh.

"Yes, it certainly is," she agreed. "I have six little sisters, and there is very little peace in our house."

"Six sisters! Christ, that sounds very trying indeed."

"It is. Do not misunderstand me, I love them all, but as the eldest, I find that I share quite simply everything with them and have so little time to myself."

"I have a younger brother, Lewis, but he's not so bad. He's a boy, so I suppose it makes it easier. I don't think I would know what to do with a little sister." His puzzled face made her giggle.

"Sisters aren't that much different from brothers, I shouldn't think. I rather imagine the challenge is the number, not the gender."

"You could be right there," Nathan said, and then he crowed as he started to pull the line on the fishing pole. "We've got one! Here!" He pressed the pole into her hands, and when the fish gave a surprisingly sharp tug, she stumbled forward. Nathan's hands caught her waist, holding her firm.

"That's it, Thea, now use the reel to bring it in. No need to worry—I've got you."

His hands upon her waist and the feel of him holding her set something in motion that she knew she was perhaps a little too young to understand fully, but she knew enough—enough to know she was going to fall in love with this handsome boy.

The fish came flopping out of the water into the shallows, and they rushed to catch it in a net.

"Oh, must we take it back? Couldn't we let it go?" she suddenly asked Nathan as he removed the hook from its mouth. For some reason, she needed this moment to be forever remembered by life, not death.

He raised his gaze to hers, studying her. "Let it live another day? Yes, I agree." He lifted the fish up and carried it deeper into the water and set it with infinite gentleness back into the river. It splashed and shot away beneath the rushing waves.

The days passed in a blinding blur, the way time speeds up quicker and quicker during the best moments of one's life. It was a thought that Thea would have every so often over the next few years as she and Nathan grew closer and closer, their secret meetings in the woods, at the stream, and eventually her family's orchards becoming so common that she spent more time with him than with her own family.

On one such afternoon when she was seventeen, she'd snuck away from her house and lay beneath the spreading branches of the cherry blossom trees. Nathan lay beside her, his body propped up against the trunk. Her head lay in his lap, and she gazed up at the blossoming branches, admiring the bright pinks and pale whites of the petals against the deep-blue summer sky.

"Thea . . . ," Nathan began uncertainly.

"Yes?"

"May I kiss you?" he asked with such sweet uncertainty that she knew she would never deny him anything. She just never imagined that someday the cost of one of his requests would be to break her own heart.

"Kiss me?" She slowly sat up, her face close to his.

"Yes." He cleared his throat. "It is what people do when they are in love."

"Are we . . . in love?" Her breath quivered in her lungs as she held herself very still.

"I am in love with you. Do you love me?" He cupped her cheek, his gaze searching hers, and she was lost in his eyes, thinking of that first day she'd seen him by the river. She had loved him every moment, waking and asleep, since that day.

"I do."

He waited for no other words, but leaned in and claimed her lips sweetly, passionately. She had never been kissed before, but she seemed to know what to do, moving her mouth with his, and soon the kiss built to something bright and wonderful that became in that moment a memory that extended into the infinite space around them.

She desperately tried to burn everything about this kiss into her memory—the feel of his warm, insistent mouth, the feel of his hand as he held her face, the way the wind blew his hair across her fingers as she dug her hands into the strands, and the dizzy bliss of knowing that he loved her.

When their mouths finally parted, they continued to stay in each other's arms, his forehead touching hers as they both sought to regain their breath.

"Thea, would you . . . wait for me?" he asked.

"Wait for you?"

"Yes. I cannot yet offer marriage, but I believe when I am twenty that I shall be able to. I don't wish for you to miss your coming out, but I fear any other decent man out there will wish to court you, and you belong to me."

"Just as you belong to me," she reminded him with an impish grin.

"Yes," he laughed. "I do, my heart, I do. More than I shall ever belong to anyone." He studied her face. "So will you . . . wait for me? Give me one year of a secret engagement so that I might propose to you properly next year?"

"Yes." There was simply no other answer she could have wished to give. She didn't want to wait even a year, but if they tried to marry now, her father probably wouldn't allow it. Eighteen was much better. As always, Nathan had carefully thought this out.

"Good," he murmured before capturing her mouth again. This time his kisses were more urgent, as though some part of him seemed to sense the doom that was coming for them both, not that she or Nathan could have known the heartache that yet lay in store for them.

Thea suddenly shivered.

"Do you wish to return to the house?" he asked in concern.

"No, no, stay and hold me a minute longer." She wanted to tuck herself away in this single instant, to bury herself in this moment and never move forward.

Her heart warned her that if she let time continue its inevitable march that something, someday, would make her wish with all her heart that she'd never moved beyond this moment. But that was life, wasn't it? Life's best moments were never permanent, and the only way not to long for the past was to pray and search for those future moments that might rival the past in all its golden glory.

5

C*hristmas Eve 1821*

A DREAM. THEA WAS STUCK IN A DREAM, ONE SHE'D had so often over the last eight years. The room was always full of people, moving and dancing. She and Nathan were at opposite ends, standing still, waiting, always too far to reach for each other or to speak. Had she fallen asleep on the coach ride to Pemberton Hall? Surely this wasn't real.

It felt too vivid to be anything but a dream. Her heart pitched straight down into her stomach. Eight years. Had it been that long? She hadn't forgotten one moment of their past. She hadn't forgotten his kisses, the tender way he'd looked at her, the softness of his smile, his hands rough and insistent on her skin as they'd melted into each other. She hadn't forgotten their conversations, the wit and intelligence of their shared thoughts or the way they could speak without words. Yet covering it all was the gray, all-consuming despair of her life when he'd left it.

Seeing him now, after all these years, the pain came rushing back to the surface, threatening to drown her. She bit her bottom lip, eyes burning with unshed tears. Instantly, she was back in the orchard, Nathan reaching for her but then drawing back before his hands could touch her. Nothing could undo the pain of his severing their connection. His father hadn't approved of her. She wasn't *suitable*. It didn't matter that her father was a well-liked country gentleman, or that she had a sizeable dowry. Nothing had pleased the old duke. Especially not her.

In the end, Nathan had listened to his father's threats against her family. She could not fault him for that—her family never knew that Nathan's noble heart had saved them that day. It would have been possible to run away with him and marry in secret, but it would have destroyed her father's life and ruined her mother's and sisters' lives as well.

Since that day she hadn't looked at another man,

hadn't been able to bear the idea of another suitor's touch. It didn't matter that she'd vowed to marry someone else, to go on to live a happy life. Nathan was her *only* love, and she'd lost him. Her hands ached to touch his face, to feel the muscles of his shoulders beneath her palms, to taste his lips and let his body warm hers. Heat infused her cheeks as, across the room, Nathan's lips formed a bittersweet smile. And just like that she was fourteen again, entrusting her heart and soul to the dashing young heir to a dukedom.

The room seemed to be suddenly devoid of air. She couldn't breathe.

He crossed the dance floor, and just as he reached her, fate intervened in the form of their host, Sir Giles.

The ruddy-cheeked gentleman grinned and clapped his hands together. "By God, it's good to see you, Hastings. The wife's been worried sick you wouldn't show tonight. I told her you would. I said, 'Mary, the boy will come. He has never turned us down yet for an invitation.' And look, here you are!" Sir Giles clapped a hand on Nathan's shoulder, seeming not to notice that Nathan's eyes had never left Thea's face.

"Yes, it was a bit snowy to travel in, Sir Giles, but I am glad to be here tonight, more than I can say."

Nathan's voice was far deeper than it had been eight years ago, such was the vast difference between a young man of twenty and a man of twenty-eight. He had grown even taller, his shoulders broader. His body warned of brute strength, despite the gentleness in his eyes as he looked at her.

"And I see you've found Miss Swann. Very good, very good. You're in time for the next dance, you two." Sir Giles reached for Thea's hand and placed it in Nathan's before he shooed them toward the dance floor.

They moved almost as though in a dream toward the floor where the other couples were lining up. The orchestra began to play a waltz, and Nathan pulled her into his arms. She tilted her face up to stare at him, half in wonder and half in fear. Eight years' worth of tears and words unspoken held her silent as they began to dance. She had thought him a marvelous dancer all those years ago when they'd practiced beneath the cherry blossoms, but now . . . now she saw that they'd both been clumsy children then. This was a true dance, their bodies moving perfectly in time as though for the last eight years they had danced together every day.

He held her without words, his eyes conveying a rush of emotions that matched the rippling waves of her own changing feelings as she tried to survive being in his arms again. It was as though this moment had been designed by the Fates to kill her with joy and sorrow at the same time. She knew her parents would see her, along with her sisters and dozens of other guests. Would they see her heart breaking all over again as it had that day?

"I'd forgotten how well you dance," Nathan said quietly.

Lord, how she'd missed his voice. It was a funny thing to lose both the love of one's life and one's dearest friend. For that was what they'd been, so much more than simply a pair of children in love. Their souls had recognized each other for mates that long-ago day by the river, and that bond had only ever strengthened. Even now it bound her to him, drowning as they both were in misery and pleasure.

"You . . ." She wasn't sure what she wanted to say, or what she *could* say without crying.

"Is . . . is your husband here?" he asked.

Husband? Yes, the thing she'd vowed to find yet hadn't been able to bring herself to. She'd broken her promise to him.

"No," she said quietly. She had no husband, so it wasn't a falsehood.

"Oh . . ." He spun her delicately, and they whirled around until the gilded light above them seem to fill every corner of the ballroom, erasing all shadows.

As the dance ended, they were greeted by numerous guests, all vying for Nathan's attention. He tried to keep hold of her hand, but she was too clever as she let the other guests step between them. Her fingers slipped from his grasp, and she was able to escape before anything else need be said.

"Thea?" Lewis called out as she rushed past him, but she didn't stop. She'd promised one dance with Nathan, and now she could be free—free to pick up the pieces of her heart all over again.

Frantic now for a quiet darkness to lose herself in, she slipped past the guests and made a hasty exit toward the doors on one side of the ballroom. Her slippered feet flew across the floor, in the direction of the door leading to Sir Giles's gardens, her sanctuary.

She pressed her palms on the wood door and pushed. A shocking, cold gust of wind cut across her collarbones and the tops of her breasts. Beyond was a terrace overlooking the now dormant gardens. The cold air cleared her head, and she felt better immediately. The stillness, the snowy quiet of the dark world around her, created a sense of peace and eased her anxious heart. She was safe. She was alone. No one would hear her cry.

A shaky breath escaped her as she felt the sobs rising up within her.

"Thea." A deep baritone voice rippled over her skin. Her spine stiffened, and she slowly pivoted.

Nathan.

She peeped up at him through her lashes and hastily dropped her gaze to the snow-covered stones.

He cleared his throat as though uncertain where to begin.

"I didn't have a chance to speak with you after the dance."

She stared at him, wordless.

"It is good to see you again. You look well." The hint of uncertainty in his voice was odd.

He'd always been so self-assured, so confident. Even in that moment when he'd broken them apart, he'd been set in his path. This new side to him confused her. She raised her eyes again. He was different, yet the same. He was still the man she'd loved with wild abandon, but age had wrought tiny lines at the corners of his eyes, and melancholy had thinned his once bewitching smile.

"Thank you. You look well too." A shiver racked her body, and she wrapped her arms around her waist.

He shrugged out of his coat. She retreated a step when he advanced on her, his coat extended.

His lips pursed, and his eyes narrowed. "Don't be silly, Thea. Let me . . ." He cornered her against the stone rail of the terrace. She jumped when wet snow pressed into her lower back, soaking through her dress. Nathan seized on her distraction and wrapped his coat around her shoulders. He surrounded her.

She didn't dare move lest he vanish as he always had in her dreams.

The smell of him, the woodsy scent with a hint of leather and horses, made her suddenly long for the past, before they'd been separated. Too wrapped in the delicious bittersweet memories of other days when he'd held her close, she didn't fight when he pushed her arms into the sleeves and pulled his coat closed to keep her warm.

It was wonderful to have the black coat around her, the warm fabric far more suitable to guard against the chill than the thin silk of her gown. But it was more than that. The coat was a shield against the present, letting her relive the past. She closed her eyes, absorbing the heat, his scent, the rush of longing. It stung, but the pain of her ache for him was beautiful. Beautiful in its tragedy.

"Thea . . ." Nathan's hands settled on her shoulders, his firm grip demanding she open her eyes. He was so close, and something tugged deep in her abdomen, beseeching her to move nearer.

"Yes?"

"I . . ." He seemed to be at a loss for words. His eyes strayed away from her face and then darted back. "You are more beautiful than the last time I saw you."

He'd once thought she was beautiful, but he'd loved her for more than that. Was he being kind so as to not make a scene? If so, then why had he followed her out here? Frustration and desperation warred inside her. She couldn't succumb to his charms, not again, not if she wanted to stay sane. She couldn't allow him back into her life, not a moment longer.

She managed a watery smile. "Don't, Nathan! You don't have to say anything. We're past that. It's been eight years. I don't need pretty words or eloquent speeches. We've seen each other. We've been cordial. We don't have to do anything else. You ought to go back inside. I'm sure there's more than one lady eager to dance with the Duke of Hastings."

Nathan's fingers dug into her shoulders, and he glared down at her with a violent emotion she couldn't read. He pressed close enough that the heat of him made her dizzy. She was on the verge of wilting in his arms.

He blinked, seemed to regain his composure, and stepped back. "So that is what you think of me." The incredulity and resignation on his face sent her heart skittering wildly. "You think I could ever love another woman the way I love you?"

Surely he didn't . . . he couldn't . . .

But he'd said *love*, not *loved*. Thea opened her mouth but didn't know what to say. She was too scared to hope, to pray that it wasn't too late.

She gasped—as much with a thrill as with surprise —when he impulsively wound his arms around her waist and hauled her against his body. Anyone could come upon them, yet he was acting rashly, something she knew he rarely did except when his heart was in control of his mind. Her heart slammed in her chest, anticipation heating her cheeks as he dipped his head and captured her mouth.

6

The kiss was everything she feared and loved. It was raw, punishing, glorious. He made up for all the days they'd been apart, all the nights she'd hungered, alone and cold without his body against hers. He slid one hand into her hair at the base of her neck and fisted his fingers in the loose ringlets, tugging at the curls. The small bite of pain spurred a flash of wet heat between her legs. She moaned against his marauding lips. As if encouraged by her wanton reaction, he slanted his mouth harder over hers. It overwhelmed her, aroused her, clouded her senses with him and only him.

The kiss was deep, their tongues dueling and lips bruising. His other hand traced her spine and skipped down to shape the curve of her rear. He clenched her bottom hard and jerked her body up several inches, setting her on the terrace balustrade.

Nathan's hands dug at her skirts, working them up her legs and out of the way so he could slide his hips between her thighs. Mindless of the cold that should have bothered her from such exposure, she arched into him, her body in control, her mind surrendering. He rocked his hips against hers, promising the passion to come with low growls against her lips as they finally broke apart from their kiss.

He stared down at her, still holding her prisoner against the terrace railing. Their shared breath formed pale clouds around their flushed faces. Nathan's lips were parted, the faint rasp of his panting sending new flashes of heat and awareness skating over her skin. Even eight years ago, they hadn't kissed like that. So much had changed, and so much lay between them. Pain, sorrow, loneliness, regret. Her barely healed heart started to crack and splinter into diamond shards, yet she wouldn't have taken that kiss back. They'd spoken with their lips, needing no words.

How did they go on from here? How did they go back to their separate lives? She was terrified of what the answer might be. She knew she wouldn't survive if he walked away a second time. There was nothing so cruel in this world than to have her heart's unattainable desire so close and for it to be denied a second time.

Destiny could not be so cold.

Nathan cupped her face in his hands and feathered his lips over hers before touching his nose to hers in a gentle nuzzle.

"God, I've been such a fool, Thea." His voice was low and pained, tinged with husky frustration.

Her throat closed, and her breath froze in her chest. Her fingers clenched and unclenched in the folds of his snowy cravat as she struggled to understand what he meant. Did he regret their kiss?

She choked back a sob. "Nathan, please. If you mean to leave, for heaven's sake, go now," she begged in a harsh whisper.

Her throat was raw with the violent heartbreak shaking her entire body. He was going to walk away, as he had before. She'd be alone again, save for a silvery-tinted memory of one last great kiss. A kiss she had no right to even remember with fondness. To love without expectation of such love being returned was a curse upon her soul. A tormenting flicker of impossible hope still clung to her, demanding she live these last few minutes with him as though she'd never lost him, never been wounded beyond repair.

If this was the last moment she had with him, she wanted to remember everything. His crisp shirt beneath her fingertips, the fire that ignited his eyes when she licked her lips.

"Leave?"

The shock in his hazel eyes made her knees buckle. She clung to his arms as she fell into him. Her head spun in dizzying circles.

"Yes, now that you've realized this was a mistake."

"No!" he snapped, his voice hard and cold. "I've never stopped loving you. I know you . . . have moved on, but . . . Christ. I won't touch you again. I know I shouldn't have. No, it is you who must leave me tonight. Or else I will find myself betraying the laws of God and man to claim you."

He still believed her married. She had to tell him the truth.

"Nathan . . ." Her whisper was barely audible. Her vision threatened to black out, but Nathan set his mouth to hers, silencing her. His kiss was hard at first, then his lips softened, coaxing her to respond.

"I was a fool to listen to my father when my heart told me you were mine. I only pray you have the mercy to forgive me."

Thea slid her hands up his shoulders and locked her fingers around his neck as she found the words she'd practiced a thousand times in a thousand unfulfilled dreams.

"When you love someone, forgiveness is unnecessary." As much as she had died that day he'd walked away, she had never needed to forgive him. He'd done what he'd done to protect her family, to protect her. How could she hate him for so noble, so loving an act?

His hands on her face tightened ever so slightly. "You still love me, my darling? Tell me now if you don't. Break my heart clean and swift."

The earnestness reflected in his eyes filled her with a strange elation, and warmth blossomed in her chest.

"I never stopped loving you. Even when I knew you'd never be mine, my broken heart still carried your name." She met his eyes, telling him the truth that she'd kept secret from the world for so long. "I was always yours." Even though it had felt like her ribs had been broken and each ragged breath cost her all of her soul, she'd kept breathing. Kept loving him.

"But you must listen to me, Nathan. I must tell you—"

"I know . . . tonight is all we have. I understand. I adore you for giving me just one last chance to hold you, my love." He nuzzled her throat, and her knees weakened.

"Nathan!" She shoved at his chest to get his attention. When he looked up at her, she held his gaze. "I broke the promise I made to you."

"You didn't," he rushed to reassure her. "I wanted

you to find and fall in love with another. I am not angry that you did. That was my wish."

"Foolish man!" she muttered. "I didn't fall in love. I didn't marry. That is the promise I broke to you." She held her breath, watching his eyes go wide.

"You . . . you are free?"

She nodded slowly. "Free to love you, if you'll let me." She wasn't sure if he still could or if tonight was simply about closure from the past. Could he still want her, even as old as she was?

"My God," he murmured. "My God . . ." He cupped her face, gently brushing his thumbs over her cheeks. "I'm not too late?"

"I am twenty-six, Nathan. I am no blushing young bride." She didn't want to tell him about the years she'd spent being mocked by younger ladies at balls, or the pitying looks from gentlemen as they passed her by when seeking a dance partner.

"I am twenty-eight, my love. We are both still young. How could you think I would want anyone else?"

"But what if . . ."

"Hush." He silenced her with a soft kiss that felt like snowflakes falling upon her lips. She surrendered to him.

Nathan pulled Thea back into his arms, tucking her head beneath his chin, his arms securing her in his embrace. He wasn't sure how long he held her, but he was too terrified to let go of her, lest she vanish like a phantom on the moors in winter. He'd been gifted with a second chance, and he wasn't going to make the same mistake.

She hadn't married. She was still his, truly his. How could it be true?

"Thea, I know I have changed, but I am still the boy you loved. Will you give me a second chance?"

Before she could answer, a flutter of wings and a soft cooing made him raise his head. Thea turned to look at the rail next to them. A pair of turtledoves perched next to each other. Their heads bobbed back and forth, their soulful black eyes watching Nathan and Thea. The two birds were a perfect match for each other. One dove bent and rubbed its cheek against the chest of its mate. The second dove raised a wing and settled it over his mate protectively against the chill of the night air.

"They're so lovely," Thea whispered. Her cheek rested against his chest. "A perfect Christmas present."

Nathan hugged her close and whispered into her ear, "Lucky for me they flew here of their own accord. I doubt I could have gotten them into a box for you."

Thea laughed. The weight on her shoulders eased and slowly disappeared.

"Say you will marry me, Thea, as soon as we can arrange it."

She nodded and smiled, her heart shining in her eyes. When she pressed her cheek to his and then nibbled a path to his ear, his body screamed out to finish what they'd started.

"I don't have a gift for you, Your Grace."

"This is my Christmas gift. Getting you back." He stole a kiss and would have made good use of the balustrade if a harried female voice hadn't cut through the air at just that moment.

"Theodosia Swann! What in heaven's name are you doing?" Thea's mother shrieked. Mrs. Swann and one of Mrs. Swann's friends, Lady Barrington, were watching them from the doorway. Lady Barrington let out a little giggle and covered her mouth with her hand.

"Mama!" Thea gasped, her delicate features morphing into a mask of horrified embarrassment. She clung to Nathan and buried her face against his chest as though to banish her mother and Lady Barrington and simply not see them.

Nathan cleared his throat and patted Thea's back in a show of silent support.

"Good evening, Mrs. Swann, Lady Barrington." He gave the two women one of his more charming smiles. It must have been ineffective after not being used for years, as Mrs. Swann didn't melt the way he'd expected her to after finding her daughter in the arms of a duke.

"Good evening, Your Grace." She arched one brow, her slightly plump arms crossed. "I trust you will be speaking to my husband later tonight about Thea's hand?"

Nathan nodded hastily.

"Excellent. What a relief this is. Seven daughters. Seven! Not one married until now. Thank heavens for mistletoe." She jabbed an imperious finger in the air. Nathan and Thea looked up. The doorway a few feet away had a large bough of mistletoe nailed to the frame. Neither he nor Thea had noticed its very obvious placement. They'd been too distracted by the drama of their reunion.

"You must come inside before you catch a cold. Thea, you should dance with His Grace again. I'm sure everyone will want to see you together now that you are to be married. *Finally*," Mrs. Swann added heavily at the end, shooting an unimpressed look at Nathan.

He felt like a boy stealing candied chestnuts from the kitchen. Clearly he would spend the next several years working his way into his future mother-in-law's good graces. He actually looked forward to the opportunity.

Thea slid her hand into his, her fingers lacing between his own. He raised their joined hands to his lips and brushed a kiss over her knuckles.

"Well, I'd better go speak with your father," he murmured as they followed Mrs. Swann and Lady Barrington back inside.

"Let me speak to him first," Thea whispered.

"I suppose that's a good idea. I doubt he's forgiven me for breaking your heart." Nathan didn't relish the idea of facing Mr. Swann, but it was the right thing to do. He squared his shoulders, and with Thea on his arm, he was ready to face anything that came, even a rightly furious future father-in-law.

7

Thea was trembling as she and Nathan entered Pemberton Hall together, arm in arm. The tongues would begin to wag the moment they were spotted, but she didn't care. After all these years, the loneliness. She had the other half of her heart back.

"Your father is this way," her mother said more gently now that they were indoors.

They entered the edge of the ballroom, and Thea spotted her father.

"I'll go and fetch him," her mother said. "Wait here."

Nathan leaned in to whisper to her. "Why do I feel so bloody nervous?"

"Because you know he's going to be angry. That's why I must speak to him first."

Thea watched her mother stop her father in the middle of a conversation, and their heads touched briefly as they shared a hushed conversation, then her father spun to look toward them.

"Oh dear," she murmured at the black look upon her father's face.

"Oh dear indeed," Nathan echoed.

Her father stormed toward them, sending dancers scattering as he crossed the middle of the ballroom floor. Everyone looked at him in confusion, but he didn't seem to care.

"Hastings," he greeted gruffly, but there was no warmth in his tone.

"Mr. Swann," Nathan replied.

"I hear you seek a private audience with me?" Her father finally looked her way.

"He does. But, Papa, I must speak with you first. I insist upon it."

"Very well. Sir Giles won't mind us using the library." He led Thea and Nathan to the library, and then after Thea followed him inside, her father shut the door in Nathan's face.

"My dear girl," her father said more gently. "What is this about marriage? When your mother said she'd found you two . . . er . . . reacquainting yourselves, I didn't quite believe her."

"I needed to speak with you to tell you what

happened that day eight years ago when Nathan came to the house to propose to me."

"I'm listening." Her father leaned against one of the nearest reading tables, his arms crossed.

"He'd gone to his father that morning seeking permission to ask me to marry him, and the old duke said no. Not only that but he threatened our family, Papa. He threatened to buy up your debts—which, if you recall, at the time were fairly significant—and he said he would throw Mama and my sisters out into the cold to . . . earn their living in what ways they could. When Nathan was told this, he knew he couldn't marry me, for the sake of you and everyone else in our family. He told me the truth that day—he never kept it from me—but it didn't make losing him any easier. I don't know how many times I wished in vain that he had broken my heart because he was a cruel man, not a noble one. It would have been easier to forget, to move on if that had been the case, but it wasn't." She had spent the last eight years on meaningful work for the poor, as well as helping manage her sisters and spending time with her friends. It had been a good life, but it wasn't complete without Nathan.

Her father was silent a long moment. "And now that old Hastings is dead, the year of mourning is up, and he's come for you."

"That's just it, Papa. He didn't know I was unwed.

He made me vow to marry another, to love another, but you know I couldn't. I saw him tonight, and it was as though I were eighteen again. It was the same for him. We spoke out on the terrace, and I told him that I hadn't married." She blushed at how quickly things had led to that explosive kiss, but she didn't dare share that with her father. "He proposed immediately."

"And that was when your mother found you . . ."

"Yes."

"Thea, you are my darling girl, the first of that wild brood of sisters. You know how deeply I love you. I simply cannot part with you to any man, not until I'm certain of your happiness."

"I know." Her throat constricted. "Seeing him tonight, brought me such unspeakable joy. I cannot tell you now how I feel knowing that the dreams that held the pieces of my heart together all these years will now come true. It's as though my entire soul is bathed in the most glorious light." Kissing Nathan, being in his arms, had chased away every shadow of the past that lay between them.

Her father blinked rapidly and rubbed at his eyes. "Well, I can't stand in the way of that, now can I?"

"You could, but you won't." She sniffled and tried to smile.

"My darling girl," he said again and cupped her cheek. "What will I do in the house when it's only your mother and sisters?" he teased her, and she laughed.

"You will laugh and roll your eyes, as you've always done. Besides, Nathan's home is so very close."

"It is, thank God for that." He sighed. "All right, let me speak to the boy."

Thea was the one who rolled her eyes this time. "He's twenty-eight, Father. He's not a boy."

"As long as I'm still alive, and therefore older, he's a damned boy." Her father's gruff tone was more playful than not.

Thea stepped into the hallway and found Nathan pacing on the oriental rug in the corridor.

"Everything go all right?" he asked.

"Yes, he'll see you now."

Nathan swiftly kissed her, and with a charming smile, he stepped into the library and closed the door.

Thea pressed herself against the door, attempting —and failing—to hear the words spoken between the two men she loved most.

"Thea?"

She spun at the sound of Lewis's voice. "Oh, Lewis, you frightened me."

He chuckled as he joined her at the closed door. "I say, are you eavesdropping? Who's inside?"

Thea stifled a giggle. "It's your brother—and my father."

"Nathan and your . . . By God, tell me the news is good?"

"The news is very good," she assured him.

Lewis's eyes lit up with joy. "Brilliant, absolutely brilliant. I'm so glad to hear that." Then he winked. "Didn't I tell you to have just one dance with him?"

Thea looked up at him. "Did you know he thought I had married?"

"I thought he knew you hadn't married—but then again, we never spoke of you. It wasn't allowed while Father was alive. And after he passed, Nathan did so very little talking at all to anyone. It was a bloody miracle I even got him to come to this ball tonight."

Thea clutched Lewis's hands. "If you hadn't, we might never have . . ." She couldn't bear to finish the thought. He seemed to realize it too.

"But he came. And everything is going to be well now, isn't it?"

"Yes." Her eyes burned with fresh tears. "It is."

The door to the library opened, and Nathan stepped out and caught sight of them.

"Ah, brother, I hear congratulations are in order?" Lewis held out a hand.

"Indeed they are. In fact, we have, with some persuasion, the ability to be married tomorrow on Christmas Day." He turned to Thea. "Your father didn't think you would mind a quick wedding. I don't wish to wait another minute, and while I can't get to

London for a special license, I can certainly pay the local church for a new roof, perhaps, or new hymnals —something that will let us skip the banns."

"I don't mind a quick ceremony. I think I brought a suitable gown, but I'll need to speak with my mother to make sure."

"Excellent." Nathan held out his hand. "Now, with that settled, I believe I'm owed a fair dozen dances."

"Won't that set the gossipers on fire?" she asked.

"Undoubtedly, but since we are to be married upon the morrow, I think we have no reason to worry." Nathan's smile was so warm, making her feel strangely flushed. She hadn't seen that smile in eight years. It was a smile of teasing mischief, of love and adoration all rolled into one charming expression.

"Come, Miss Swann. We must dance."

And dance they did, for the next hour until their feet were sore and their faces hurt from smiling so much. Sir Giles stilled the orchestra for a moment and announced that the coaches were all trapped and that no one would be able to leave tonight, and all were welcome to stay in his home, the rooms of which were bountiful in number.

"Snowed in for Christmas." Thea sighed dreamily as she leaned against Nathan's arm. "How perfectly splendid."

"Splendid indeed." He led her out of the ballroom with the other guests, and she met her mother and sisters in the throng of people at the base of the stairs.

"I'll see you tomorrow morning, my love." Nathan bent and pressed a kiss to her hand before she was ushered upstairs by her mother.

She paused one last time to gaze down at him, her heart stilling for a beat too long. How different tonight had been than what she'd expected. She'd left her home with a broken heart, and now, amidst the merry cheer of the season, she'd been given a second chance at joy. It was a thought that would play over and over again as she climbed into bed with the snow falling outside.

⚜ 8 ⚘

Christmas morning was snowy with overcast skies as Thea, bundled in a bright yellow-gold cloak, exited the coach that had carried her to the small church abutting Sir Giles's property. She pushed back the hood as she walked up the church steps with her father.

Neither of them said a word, both too afraid to speak lest either of them let emotions run away with them. Her father simply sighed with a sad smile and patted her hand as he led her inside and then removed her cloak, handing it to one of Sir Giles's footmen who had accompanied them.

"Let's get you married, eh?" her father said as they stood at the end of the long aisle leading up to the alter. Nathan was watching her, Lewis at his side.

She walked toward him, her heart humming with

a quiet but infinite joy. Her father kissed her cheek and stepped back so that she could stand beside Nathan and speak her vows. They were pronounced man and wife to the cheers of the guests, who had all attended the ball the previous night. There were murmurs of how lovely a Christmas Day wedding was, how romantic. Thea had to agree. The holidays used to be her favorite time of the year, but after losing Nathan, she'd lost the joy of Christmas too. But now—now she had the magic of the holidays back.

The festivities of the day were a delightful blur of laughter, the wedding breakfast, cake, and general celebrations. The men went in search of a Yule log, while the ladies sipped hot cider and warmed themselves by the fire. After a few hours, the men came tramping past the window, singing and laughing as they dragged a large log behind them. Sir Giles was in the lead, his baritone voice leading them in Christmas carols.

Thea giggled at the sight of Nathan and Lewis both joining in the fun. She blushed as she thought that in a few precious hours she would soon be spending her wedding night with him.

Dinner was a lavish affair, with carved turkey, figgy puddings, cranberry relish, and several other courses that left Thea quite satisfied, but her stomach was still quivering with nerves as she prepared for bed a short while later. Many of the guests weren't ready yet to retire, but the men had set about teasing Nathan that he needed to see to his marital duties straightaway. So it was with delighted embarrassment that she and Nathan, hand in hand, went up to bed together.

Lady Pemberton's lady's maid saw to helping her undress and pulling her hair down from her coiffure.

"You'll be fine, miss," the girl promised before flashing Thea an encouraging smile and taking her leave.

Thea vaguely knew what to expect tonight, but it didn't make her any less nervous. She nearly jumped when Nathan knocked on the bedchamber door.

"Come in," she called out. She stood near the bed, twining her hands fitfully in her nightgown. He entered her room, wearing sleeping trousers and a dark-red banyan wrapped around him.

"How are you feeling?" he asked as he came toward her and gently pried her anxious fingers from the nightgown.

"Nervous," she admitted. It was a strange thing to feel so shy toward him now after all this time, after everything they'd been through, yet eight years apart had taken so much of her physical confidence from her when it came to being alone with him.

"Never say so," he teased with a twinkle in his eyes. "Not my Thea. Wasn't it you who scaled the wall of old Mr. Adams's gardens to steal his raspberries? I was a damned sight more afraid than you were."

She giggled. "I did do that, didn't I?" Some part of her had forgotten what she'd been like as a young girl, how she'd been wild and carefree.

"Yes, and I promise tonight will be far better than that."

"Is that so?" She tilted her head and shot him a purposely saucy look.

He chuckled, and before she could react, he swept her up in his arms and laid her gently down upon the bed.

"Now, let us agree for neither of us to be startled by what we discover tonight."

"What *we* discover? What do you mean?"

"I mean, my darling, that I also have not done . . . *this* before."

Thea stared at her husband. "You . . . you are a virgin too?" she blurted out, then covered her mouth with her hand.

"Er . . . yes, I am." He looked down at the floor, seeming to study the carpet quite intensely, as though it held the secrets of the universe.

She sat up on the bed and caught hold of one of his hands.

"But how?" she asked.

"How?" He seemed confused by the question.

"Yes, why didn't you . . . Surely there were other women who wanted . . ."

"There were plenty, but not one of them was you. I had ample opportunities over the years, but my heart and body were not interested." He squeezed her hand gently. "So we shall explore this together." He raised her hand to his chest, and she slid her palm beneath the opening of the banyan. With artful slowness, she pushed it off his shoulders. He let the dressing gown fall to the floor so that he stood bare-chested before her.

It wasn't the first time she'd seen him half naked. When they'd played by the river, she'd seen him in breeches and nothing else quite often, but this was so different—he was so different now. There were harder lines of muscle, a larger frame to his body. While she continued to stroke his chest, he swept her hair back from her neck and ran his fingertips up and down the column of her throat, as though similarly mesmerized.

"How is it possible that you are even more beautiful than you were at eighteen?" he asked.

She lowered her chin, strangely embarrassed. "I'm not. I am so much older . . ."

"Age doesn't matter. You are still in the blush of youth, my love, and you will always be beautiful to me, more so with each year." He tilted her face up and leaned in to kiss her.

It was the sort of kiss she'd first expected upon the terrace—soft, full of sunny secrets, and almost unbearably sweet. She parted her lips, letting his tongue dance with hers, and a heat uncoiled deep in her belly. She dropped her legs off the side of the bed and pulled her nightgown up to her hips so that she could part her legs and let him step closer.

"My darling love," he murmured as he cupped her face in his hands.

They kissed for what felt like hours before he helped her remove her nightgown and he shed his sleeping trousers. They climbed into bed together, lying side by side, neither of them rushing this moment. He held on to her hip with one hand, his thumb stroking lightly back and forth as he simply stared at her and she at him. Her hair fell in waves around her breasts, half hiding them from his view, but he didn't seem to mind. He picked up one of the coils of her hair, spooling it around one finger.

"This doesn't quite seem real, does it?" he asked.

She laughed softly. "No, it doesn't. But I rather wish to stay here with you, even if it is a dream."

"Me too." He wrapped his arm around her and leaned over her so that she lay back upon the bed.

Nathan slid between her thighs, settling his weight atop her, and it felt good, his warmth and hardness above her and the soft mattress below.

When he kissed her again, she was lost in the

taste of him, the feel of his lips exploring hers. There was no desperation this time, only a playful eagerness that put her at ease. She tensed a little as he entered her body, and the pinch of pain made her gasp against his lips.

"I'm sorry," he murmured. "It will never happen again," he promised.

Nathan held his hips still, his body trembling slightly as he kissed her neck and nibbled that spot in the curve of her neck and shoulder that made her giddy and flushed. She raised her hips to his, encouraging him to move.

"Nathan, you must move. I think I shall die." She was quite certain something infinitely wonderful was so close to the surface within her, but she was afraid she'd lose it if he didn't move.

His laughter rumbled through her. "I'm afraid if I do move, *I* might die, but let it be said I'll never deny you anything." He lifted his hips away, his shaft drawing out of her almost entirely before he thrust back in, and the sudden fullness made her breath catch. She curled her arms around his neck clinging to him as he rode her slowly, taking his time until she was moaning in desperation beneath him.

"Please, Nathan, you are torturing me." She dug her fingertips into his shoulders, urging him on. He answered with faster movements, thrusting harder, deeper, until she felt a feeling of physical perfection that swelled within her, and she cried out as it came to a blinding peak. Then she simply shattered and fell away into the dust of pleasured dreams. Nathan continued to move a second or two longer, and then he stiffened and hoarsely cried out her name.

They collapsed on the bed in a tangle of limbs and sated smiles.

"Was it everything you hoped for?" she asked him.

"It was . . . something beyond compare to anything I've ever experienced. What about you?" he asked with concern. "Did I hurt you too much?"

"No." She smiled and cupped his face. "There was only a little at the beginning, and the end . . ." She blushed. "Well, I want to do that again very soon, husband."

"Insatiable minx," he teased and kissed the tip of her nose. "Give me a moment to recover myself, and I shall oblige you, my love." He pulled back the blankets of their bed, and they both crawled underneath them.

Nathan tucked her into his arms, and she rested her chin on his chest with a contented sigh.

"Is it strange to say that I feel as though I could sleep a hundred years? I feel that at peace right now." She pressed a kiss to his chest, so much more comfortable now with his nakedness and her own than she'd ever imagined she could be.

"Me too." He stroked her hair. "I felt lost in a

storm for so long that it's hard to trust the shore I've landed upon, yet it feels sturdy beneath my feet."

"Mine too." She offered a lazy grin that made him laugh.

They lay together for a while before making love a second time. When it was nearing midnight, the moonlight suddenly appeared so bright and white upon the balcony of their room that it was as clear as daylight.

"Let me go shut the curtains." Nathan slipped out of bed and pulled on his dressing gown against the chill. Then he moved to the balcony. Drawn to follow him, she gathered her own dressing gown, which lay over the back of a chair, and she joined him at the windows.

Wrapping an arm around her, he pulled her against his side as they stared out into the snowy moonlit world.

"Will you be happy with me?" he asked.

"Deliriously happy. And you?" She crinkled her nose in concern.

"Ridiculously happy." He stroked a fingertip down the length of her upturned nose, winning a genuine smile from her petal-soft lips.

"We are fools in love."

The hazel hue of Nathan's eyes was so heated that it made her heart gallop at an uneven pace.

"Lucky fools," he agreed.

They'd wasted so much time without each other. But never again. They'd never let each other go.

As he started to pull the curtain closed, she caught a glimpse of two turtledoves resting on the edge of the balcony railing. She sensed they were the same pair from the terrace overlooking the gardens where she and Nathan had been reunited. The two doves cuddled into each other. One dove's eyes were closed, the other's at half-mast, as though lost in the pleasure of simply being close to its mate. They seemed happy, as happy as two creatures made for each other could be. Thea knew exactly how they felt. She tucked herself into Nathan's side as he turned back toward bed, with a heart so light it threatened to float away upon a light breeze. Nathan took her in his arms and claimed her mouth with a kiss that promised only good things to come, and as she dreamed that night of her future, she saw the two of them, nestled together like the turtledoves.

On the second day of Christmas, my true love gave to me, two turtledoves and a love everlasting.

THANK YOU SO MUCH FOR READING THE DUKE'S Dove! I hope you'll check out the next book in the series A Fowl Christmastide by Sandra Sookoo!

*Don't miss a new release from me by going to

my website at www.laurensmithbooks.com and doing the following:

Follow me on BOOK BUB !

Sign up for my NEWSLETTER !

TURN THE PAGE TO READ THE FIRST THREE chapters of Seducing an Heiress on a Train where a young heiress falls for a desperate fortune hunter while traveling to Scotland for Christmas!

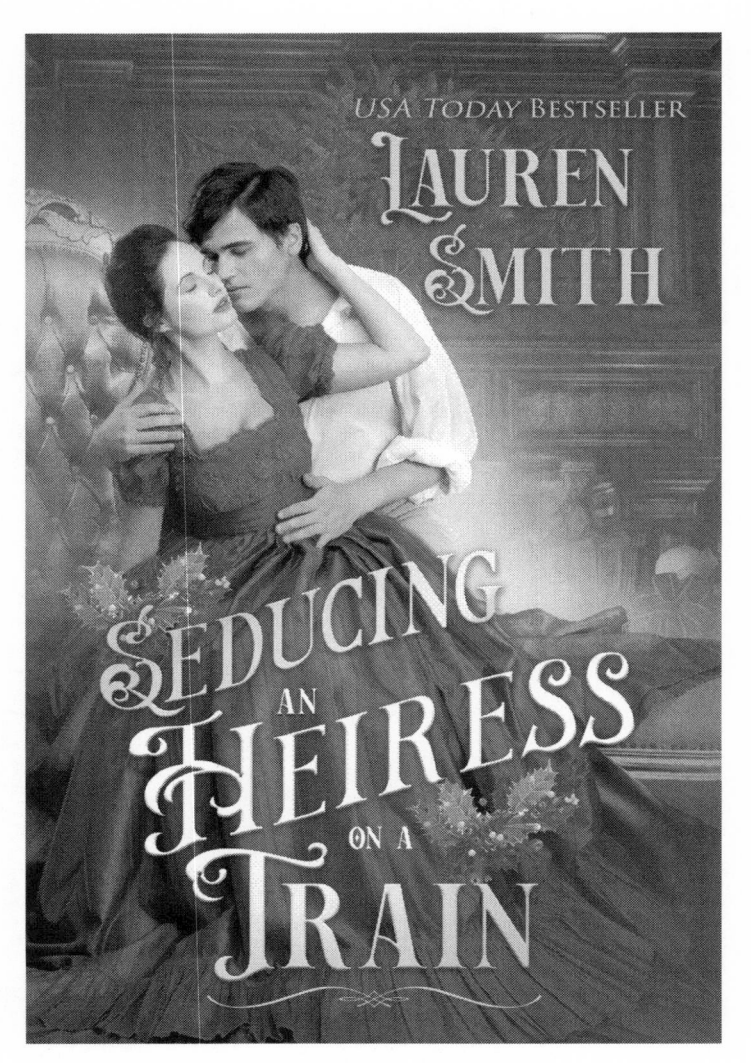

USA TODAY BESTSELLER

LAUREN SMITH

SEDUCING AN HEIRESS ON A TRAIN

SEDUCING AN HEIRESS ON A TRAIN
CHAPTER 1

London, December 1888

The ticking clock in the corner of the waiting area counted down the seconds toward Oliver Conway's doom. Each second sounded like a hammer fall in the interminable silence. He clenched his worn black gloves in one hand and held his hat in the other as he waited to be summoned. Finally, the door to the bank president's office opened, and a portly man with kind eyes glanced down the hall to find him.

"Lord Conway, I will see you now."

Oliver swallowed and stood, then straightened his shoulders and entered the office of Mr. Kelly, president of Drummonds Bank.

"Please, sit, Lord Conway." Mr. Kelly waved at the pair of leather chairs facing the desk.

Oliver sat, his hands trembling a little. At the grown age of one and thirty he had few reasons to be afraid, but today this man held the fate of Oliver's family's future in his hands.

Mr. Kelly removed a pair of spectacles from his coat pocket and nestled them on the bridge of his nose. He pulled a stack of papers toward him. "I've reviewed all of the accounts this morning, my lord, and I'm afraid the loans your father extended two years ago are past due. I received the payments you've been sending, but it barely covers the interest currently owed."

Oliver's heart sank, and a bitter taste filled his mouth. "And the stock he purchased? We authorized the bank with permission to sell. What amount did it bring in?"

Mr. Kelly sighed, and his gray eyes, still showing that damnable sincerity and kindness, only increased Oliver's fears.

"The stock was worthless after the businesses your father invested in went bankrupt. I was able to recuperate a small amount, but it covered only the interest owed for the next month's payment."

Panic spread through Oliver. He had been fighting for over a year to save his family and his home from ruin after his father's death, and now all he had was his name and the title of Viscount Conway, which at the moment was a burden almost beyond what he could bear.

"Mr. Kelly, is there no way...?"

The banker removed his spectacles and set them on the desk. He leaned forward, his voice lowering.

"I have so few options, Oliver. Your father was a dear friend and..." Mr. Kelly paused, collecting himself. "But my hands are tied by bank regulations and investor expectations."

"So that's it, then? Astley Court, all of the tenancy properties and everything we own..."

"Will be property of Drummonds in thirty days," Mr. Kelly finished. "You've done a commendable job, but the debts were simply too great. The only way to..." Mr. Kelly stopped and shook his head.

"What?" Oliver pressed. "What were you about to say? I will do anything."

"The only option I see as a way out of this mess is to, shall we say...marry advantageously?"

Oliver didn't quite comprehend the banker's words because they were so unexpected. "Pardon?"

"An heiress, dear boy," Mr. Kelly said, forgetting their difference in social standing for a moment, not that Oliver cared.

"An heiress," he muttered, finding the implication distasteful.

"Yes. Find a pretty young lady with a fortune to her name and secure her hand in less than thirty days, and you will have access to money. I could get around some of the resistance here if you returned before the middle of January with a rich bride upon your arm."

Oliver stared down at his worn-out gloves and top hat, which rested in his lap. So it had come to this. Sell himself to the highest-bidding lady in London and find himself saddled with a wife, one he might not like, let alone love—all to save his home and family.

"Do it for Astley Court. Do it for your mother."

The thought of his mother, his younger brother Everett, and his sister Zadie all depending on him. It was all it took to make him decide.

"Thirty days," Oliver said, as if sealing the pact.

Still feeling like a man doomed and facing the gallows, Oliver thanked Mr. Kelly and shook his hand before he exited the office. He pulled on his gloves and cursed as he found yet another small hole in the leather. He had spent the last year putting every bit of coin he had toward the business debts his father's investments had accrued. The cost of his efforts, aside from his pride, had been clothing three years too old, and showing every day of it.

His mother and sister had suffered more, being forced to wear gowns well out of fashion. He and Everett were able to get by on what they owned since men's fashions changed far less and more slowly than the fashions of ladies. Zadie had held her head high, even when other girls had mocked her during her debut this season when she'd worn an outmoded gown.

His family had also reduced the staff at their country estate by half and had sold their large townhouse in London six months ago. Now they only rented rooms when in town for the season. Oliver didn't want to think about what cuts they would have to make if he wasn't able to save Astley Court. A man without land and without a fortune... He shuddered, but resolved himself to the idea of learning a trade. He was not opposed to it, but the social circles his family ran in would surely find it distasteful, which meant he put Everett's and Zadie's futures at risk.

But if he could find an heiress...

No. He *would* find an heiress. He would do his duty, in whatever form that required.

As he left Drummonds and stepped out into the streets, someone called his name.

"Conway!"

He spun to find a man striding toward him, waving his arm. The tall, dark-haired fellow had the same green eyes as him.

"Cousin!" He laughed as he shook Devon St. Laurent's hand. Devon was second in line to become the Duke of Essex. Oliver's great-grandfather, Godric St. Laurent, and his wife Emily had had four children, and Devon's grandfather, second eldest of the brood, was the current duke.

"Care for a drink? I was heading to Berkley's."

"I would love to, but I surrendered my membership three months ago." It was one of the many frivolous luxuries both he and Everett had removed to slim down their family's expenses.

"What? Why?"

Oliver sighed. "It is a long story." His shoulders ached now. He had been waiting to see Mr. Kelly for over an hour, and he had been strung tighter than an archer's bow the entire time.

Devon smiled and clapped a hand on Oliver's shoulder. "Come on, we'll drink at a pub nearby, and you can tell me this long story."

Half an hour later, the two of them were two pints into a nice afternoon.

"All right, Oliver, tell me what's the matter." Devon's expression was back to that of concern. And like they had been as boys, Oliver found his trust in his cousin well placed as he shared his family's dire financial straits.

"Lord, Oliver, that's dreadful. Why don't you speak to my grandfather? I'm sure he wouldn't mind helping you out. You know how he loves Astley Court."

"I know," Oliver admitted. His great-uncle, the Duke of Essex, was a loving man, openhearted and kind, but even he did not possess the funds to help the Conways out of their massive debt.

"Why not?" Devon pressed. He rolled his half-empty pint glass between his hands.

"It wouldn't be enough. The amount we need to pay... It would put Essex House at risk. I cannot ask that."

Devon's eyes darkened. "It's truly that bad?"

"It is," Oliver replied numbly. He glanced around the pub, noting the men who sought to escape the winter chill. Most were laughing and talking, all in seemingly good spirits. It only served to deepen his melancholy.

"I feel I've failed," Oliver whispered.

"You haven't." Devon leaned forward and set his glass down on the table. "Debts happen, businesses fail. Your father made these choices, and they seemed good and sound at the time. It isn't your fault they failed. The world changed, and we're all still trying to catch up with it."

Oliver drained the rest of his pint, letting the stout ale go to his head. His stomach was empty, and his head ached from the lack of food. He had done his best not to eat at too many restaurants while he was in London. The expense was one more thing he couldn't afford.

"The banker said I need to find an heiress. Can you believe that? It was his *professional* advice."

"An heiress?" Delight suddenly burst on Devon's

face as he grinned. "That may be something I could help you with."

"Oh?"

"You remember Adelaide Berwick?"

"The Earl of Berwick's daughter?" He nodded. He had spent much of his youth around the girl. She chattered endlessly and could be quite mean-spirited sometimes.

"She still wants you, Oliver. I know you didn't offer for her when she came out last year, but she is still hoping you'll change your mind. Her father has settled a hefty sum on her as a dowry and a large sum to be given as an inheritance if he approves of the match. Old Berwick always liked you."

The Earl of Berwick was a good fellow, but his wife and his only daughter could both be unbearable. Still, Oliver considered it.

"Adelaide is a bit...much, don't you think?" he asked his cousin.

Devon shrugged. "Yes, I suppose she is. But she's as rich as Croesus, and that's what you need, isn't it?" His cousin chuckled. "Besides, if she truly drove you mad, you could always live apart in separate homes. That seems to be quite acceptable these days with those who marry out of necessity."

"I suppose you're right. I could stomach it. For Astley Court."

"There you are then. Cheer up. You're coming to

Lady Poole's ball tonight, aren't you? Adelaide will be there. Propose to her, and I'll go with you to procure a special license. You'll be married by Christmas."

"Married to Adelaide Berwick by Christmas..." Oliver shook his head, trying not to laugh at the maddening twist his life had taken.

"Married, at least," Devon replied. "That ought to be some consolation."

They finished their drinks, and Devon paid for their drinks. They then donned their gloves and hats before embracing the chill outside.

"Shall I see you tonight?"

"You shall." Oliver shook Devon's hand and parted ways with his cousin. He walked to the hotel his family were renting rooms at while they were in town. The Grosvenor Hotel on Buckingham Palace Road was an impressive structure modeled in the Baroque interpretation of French Renaissance architectural style. His father had been a good friend of the hotel's current owner, and whenever they stayed in town, they were able to rent a room far cheaper than most guests, for which Oliver was extremely grateful. It didn't hurt that having a titled lord staying there caused a flurry of interest from other guests, which the owner thought was good for business.

As Oliver entered its opulent entryway, his eyes rolled over the fluted twisting columns and the way the light from the chandeliers turned the white marble a soft gold. Bright-red roses filled half a dozen large crystal vases, and a group of young ladies in colorful gowns were gossiping as they donned their velvet manteaux, likely for an evening out at the opera or perhaps a ball. More than one lady in the group caught Oliver's eye, offering him a blushing smile before they dissolved into giggles with their friends as he passed.

In another life, Oliver would've enjoyed the attention. He was no fool. He had his mother's fair looks as well as his father's, and more than one young lady had thrown herself at him over the years. He had thoroughly enjoyed seducing a few, though never too far, just enough to please his ego and give the lady a breathtaking memory.

But he was older now, and there was a part of him that did long to settle down. He wanted what his mother and father had, a marriage based on love and respect.

But I won't have that with Adelaide. She will own me, and she'll never let me forget it.

He climbed the stairs to the third floor and then headed down the hall to the suite of rooms he'd rented. As he opened the door, he saw his mother and sister in the sitting room, talking excitedly about tonight.

"Oh, Oliver!" his mother exclaimed in joy as she saw him. She rose and came over to embrace him.

"How was Mr. Kelly? Did he give us a very long extension?"

Oliver's gut knotted as he carefully planned his response. He saw his little sister, Zadie, who was only eighteen, watching him with anxious eyes.

She knows. She's always been able to read me like an open book.

"Mother, perhaps you should sit down."

His mother, still lovely even at fifty-two, now became concerned. "Oliver... What's the matter? What did Mr. Kelly say?"

Zadie gently ushered their mother into a chair, and then she stood behind it, as strong as a soldier in Her Majesty's army.

"Where is Everett?" he asked.

"Here." His brother stepped out of the nearest bedroom. Everett could be Oliver's twin, though he was three years younger. He'd removed his coat and was waiting for Oliver to speak. They all were.

"Mr. Kelly could not grant us an extension. The entire amount of the debt has been called in, and we are destitute. We have thirty days to set our affairs in order and arrange for the sale of Astley Court and all of its sub properties, as well as the furnishings in the house."

That bitter taste had returned, and it broke his heart to see his mother wipe the tears in her eyes. No matter what Devon had said, he knew he had failed his family.

"I haven't given up," Oliver told them. "I have one last chance. Mr. Kelly suggested it, and I shall endeavor to do my best."

"What is it?" his mother asked. Even though her husband had passed more than a year ago, she, like Her Majesty, still mourned her husband and had not shed her widow's weeds. Her black silk gown was whispered against the carpets as she stood and faced him with a strength that made him proud.

"If I can marry an heiress before the middle of next January, we'll be able to save the house, tenancies...all of it."

"An heiress? Oh, Oliver, no." His mother shook her head. "I'll not have you become some dreadful fortune hunter."

"I won't be, Mother. I already know the woman I'm choosing, and she won't require any hunting." He tried to smile, but he knew the expression failed to reach his eyes. "You could even say that she's been hunting me."

"Who would be...?" Zadie asked, and then her eyes widened with horror. "Oh no, Oliver, not her. *Anyone* but her."

"Zadie." He held up a hand, trying to reassure her. "She's not that terrible."

"Not that terrible? She covered my hair in tar

when I was twelve, Oliver. Mother had to cut it all off. I looked like a boy for almost a year!"

"Bloody hell," Everett said, then whistled. "I forgot Adelaide did that."

"She was just a girl then," Oliver said.

Everett shook his head in disgust. "Choose anyone but that one. There must be other heiresses."

"Everett, heiresses do not grow on trees," their mother said coldly. "If Oliver believes Adelaide is our only choice, then we must bear it." When Everett made a gagging noise, she added, "Or *you* could marry her." At which point, Everett turned as white as alabaster.

Zadie sank into the chair their mother had now vacated, while Everett shot Oliver a sympathetic look as their mother took his hands in hers and gave a gentle squeeze.

"You truly want this?" Margaret asked him.

Oliver squeezed her hands back. "Mother, it's not what I want, but it is what must be done. I won't lose our home, and I won't put Zadie's and Everett's futures at risk. They need a stable life and a reputation unsullied by destitution if they are to make decent matches."

For a long moment, no one said anything. Then his mother cupped his cheek and tried to smile. "You are a wonderful son to make such a sacrifice. I would give anything to keep you from doing this."

"I know, Mother." He closed his eyes, drew a deep breath, and tried to summon a smile. "Now, we have Lady Poole's ball tonight, and I for one would like to enjoy myself this evening before I propose."

He would not let himself think about what his future might be. Certainly not tonight with his last night of freedom before he shackled himself to an unwanted heiress.

CHAPTER 2

Rayne Egerton tried to quell the rise of nerves that fluttered in her belly as her father helped her down from their coach. Her father, Douglas Egerton, beamed at her with pride. She tried to smile back.

"Breathe, my dear. You'll do just fine. None of these ladies are any more special than you."

Rayne wished her father's words could comfort her, but the truth was, she felt out of place in England. They had only just arrived from a steamer ship out of New York, and London was proving to be more intimidating than New York had ever been. As much as she liked the country, the people seemed far less welcoming than she'd hoped. Even Americans with all their money weren't always welcome...or perhaps it was because of it?

"It's my first English ball, Father. What if I don't know the right dances or say the wrong thing to one of the peers? The titles still confuse me." She had spent the last month reading a copy of *Debrett's Peerage* as she tried to understand the complicated system. Rayne still felt completely uncomfortable with all of the modes of address. At home, a woman was either a *Miss* or a *Mrs.*, and a man was simply a *Mr.* There were no earls, dukes, viscount, barons, or knights. Here it was all *Lord this* or *Right Honorable that*. And trying to keep their order of importance straight... It was all too much.

A footman at the door ushered them into Lady Poole's extravagant home. Great chandeliers lit the entry hall as she and her father joined the other newly arrived guests. She removed her ivory-colored silk-and-velvet dolman, something that resembled a half-coat and half-cape with its loose, sling-like sleeves. She unhooked the fastener at her neck and allowed the footman to slip it off and put it away for her. Her father had insisted on the new costly wardrobe before they had left for England. He'd had the gowns ordered from the House of Worth in Paris. It had embarrassed her to have such expensive things, but her father said they would be judged quite harshly based on their clothing. He'd reminded her that they would have to work twice as hard to fit in with the social crowd of London during the season.

To make the best impression, she had chosen a pale-rose evening gown with a low square neckline and sleeves that clung to the edges of her shoulders. Her gown was trimmed with live roses that had been carefully sewn in over the embroidered silk rosebuds on her skirts, draping from the high bustle at the back down to the front of her gown. A red silk bow exited the middle of her bustle, catching the viewer's eye to the pale-pink gown. It was exquisite, but Rayne wasn't used to such things, and she certainly didn't feel like she belonged in it.

At home in New York, she'd worn more serviceable, sensible clothes because she spent a great deal of time assisting her father at his office. She was fortunate to have a father who believed women were capable of working alongside men, but he was the exception. Most men in New York had laughed at her attempts to discuss business and politics, and she was afraid London would be no different.

As she and her father entered the ballroom, dozens of women were already eyeing her, whispering behind raised fans, their eyes glittering with curiosity or malice. She knew why—she was an American heiress, and every unattached man in the room would soon find a way to manage an introduction to her. It was a common practice now for the titled men of England to seek marriages with rich American heiresses. And that was the very last thing Rayne wanted, for a man to see her simply as a bank account. She didn't care if the man was a duke—if he was a fortune hunter, she wanted nothing to do with him.

She kept her arm tucked in her father's, and her other hand clutched her skirts as they moved through the thick crowds. There had to be close to seventy people inside the room. Musicians played in a distant corner, and waiters moved around the edges of the crowd, offering champagne to those not partaking in the dance. Rayne watched the dancers, trying to recognize the steps, wondering how best to match them. The only dance she felt comfortable with was the waltz.

"Mr. Egerton!" Lady Poole came over, beaming at them both. She had met Rayne's father a few months ago while in New York and had sent them invitations the moment she discovered they would be visiting England.

Her father bowed, and Rayne dipped into a curtsy. "Lady Poole." The fashionable English-woman was in her midforties and still quite stunning. The soft smile she cast toward Douglas didn't go unnoticed by Rayne. She'd wondered over the last year if her father and Lady Poole's frequent letters to one another might be leading to something more. If he found happiness again after losing his wife, Rayne was ready to support his decision to remarry. All the more so if he chose Lady Poole.

"How are you faring, Rayne, dear?" Lady Poole asked. Rayne smiled in genuine relief at having at least one ally here.

"A bit nervous, I admit."

"That's quite normal." Lady Poole tapped her closed fan in her palm. "Let's see if I can't make some introductions." She took Rayne from her father's arm and then towed her quickly around the room, introducing her to all the ladies in attendance. The names and titles became a confusing blur by the end.

"Stay here while I fetch some gentlemen to fill your dance card, my dear." She left Rayne at a spot near the wall with a group of other young ladies. They all shared sympathetic looks with her.

Rayne tried not to lose herself in shame as she watched a number of handsome young bucks prowl by her and the others left out of the dancing.

Heavens...I've become a wallflower so soon.

"Oh dear." The girl next to her shuffled her feet anxiously. "She's coming. Buck up, ladies," the girl hissed in warning to her fellow flowers.

"Who?" Rayne asked the girl, her stomach knotting with dread.

"Adelaide Berwick. Whatever you do, don't show any hint of weakness," the girl replied and raised her chin defiantly as a pretty young woman around

Rayne's age came up to the group of single ladies. A trio of girls followed on Adelaide's heels, all twittering behind their fans.

"Well, 'tis a pity Lady Poole did not invite more young men. Quite silly to have so many left desiring partners. There's simply *nothing* worse than being a wallflower," she declared. Her soft blue silk gown, Rayne noted, looked as expensive as hers, but it lacked the flair of the roses. Adelaide seemed to notice this and sneered at Rayne.

"I do believe you're wilting." She pointed her fan at Rayne's dress. Rayne almost looked down but didn't. Even if the freshly cut roses were wilting, she didn't want to give the girl the satisfaction. She knew how she would respond in America, but here? She was well out of her depth.

Adelaide change the subject. "I'm afraid we're not acquainted. You aren't familiar to me. Let me guess... A country cousin of Lady Poole's? She is always so charitable." Adelaide's friends giggled.

Rayne bit the side of her cheek. *Do not respond. You will embarrass Father*.

"Oh dear. Have you lost your tongue?" Adelaide continued. "The country mouse is too timid."

Rayne curled her fingers around her own fan, inwardly imagining bringing it down upon Adelaide's head.

"I have a tongue, Miss Berwick. You're simply not worth the breath or the words to speak to."

The wallflowers behind Rayne all gasped. Adelaide's brown eyes narrowed to angry slits. She tossed her auburn curls venomously.

"You are American, of course. You must be the daughter of that rich old man everyone is fussing over tonight. Well, lesson one, *American*. I'm the daughter of Lord Berwick, so you will address me as Lady Adelaide, not *miss*." Her smugness was short-lived because Rayne was good and furious now at the girl's dig at her father. No one insulted him, especially not some twit like this.

Rayne took a step closer, plastering a smile upon her face. "My apologies, Lady Adelaide. I didn't see an earl's daughter here, only a spoiled little brat."

Adelaide bared her teeth as she readied a response, but Rayne wasn't done. She raised her voice a little so the girls behind her all heard.

"Be careful what you say next, Lady Adelaide, or I might ask my father to purchase everything you own. As you said, I'm the daughter of a very rich American. My father could buy half this country on a lark if it suited him."

Adelaide's face went ghostly white, and then her pretty face pinched and her cheeks turned a bright red.

"All the money in the world doesn't fix poor breeding," she snapped.

"I suppose you would know, seeing as how most old families in England are inbred," Rayne shot back without a second thought.

Adelaide looked ready to spew fire, but the trio of girls behind her pulled her away, steering her toward the table of refreshments. Rayne released a sigh of relief.

"You Americans really are as bold as brass, as they say," the girl next to her said. She had stunning green eyes and dark-brown hair.

"I realize that may have been very foolish." Rayne blushed. Her temper was cooling, and as it did, rationality and doubt returned, along with embarrassment. She had just threatened the daughter of an earl. That wouldn't go over well.

"Could you truly do it?" the girl asked.

"Do what?" Rayne replied.

"Buy her family's estate and property like that?"

"Perhaps. What does her father earn in any given year?" She blushed again at the inappropriate question. The English thought it was so crass to talk openly of money.

"About forty thousand a year."

Rayne didn't even hesitate. "Oh yes, definitely. Twice over, I should think."

The wallflowers gathered around her then, all gasping and chattering questions all at once.

"Ladies, let her breathe," the green-eyed girl exclaimed. "My name is Zadie, by the way. It's a pleasure to meet you."

"The same," Rayne replied, relaxing a little at Zadie's warm smile. "I'm Rayne Egerton."

"Rayne, you told off Lady Adelaide, and that makes you my new favorite friend."

"I take it she terrorizes you all often?"

"Often," Zadie agreed with a frown. "She's the worst sort of aristocrat Not all ladies in her station are like that. I hope you won't judge the rest of us by her standards."

"Certainly not," Rayne promised. "I let people prove their worth before I pass judgment. And I think Adelaide proved she isn't worth anything."

The flowers flocking around her all laughed. Zadie introduced her to most of the girls, and she felt a stirring of hope that she might make a few friends tonight.

"So, how long are you in England?" Zadie asked as she and Rayne collected champagne from a passing footman.

"A few months. My father is here to buy stock in some steel companies."

"Oh? And your Christmas plans? Will you be staying in London?"

"No, we leave tomorrow by train for Inverness. Lord Fraser has invited us to a party there over the holidays."

"Lord Fraser's estate?" Zadie grinned. "I'm bound there as well. Only we leave in a few days, not tomorrow."

Rayne's heart soared. "You'll be there? Thank heavens, I'll have one friend at least."

Zadie chuckled. "Not to worry. I'll help you survive the end of the season and the holidays."

"Thank you."

"Oh!" Zadie suddenly looked toward a crowd on the opposite end of the ballroom. "I must go, I'm afraid. But I'll see you in Inverness." Zadie gave her a hug and rushed off. It was only as she watched her friend go that she noticed that Adelaide and the other girls nearby were laughing at Zadie.

She heard Adelaide say, "There's only so many ways to change the same old gown before a decent gentleman notices you can't afford a new one."

Rayne drew in a deep breath. If she wasn't careful, Adelaide might end up with her face drenched in champagne. Lord, Adelaide was testing the strength of her self-control.

Lady Poole plucked her from the wallflowers and sent her onto the dance floor. She had lined up a dozen young men to meet her. In between the twirls and whirls, they talked of her father and her holiday plans. Rayne tried her best to be clever, charming, and entertaining, and she found she wasn't a complete failure.

One man, Devon St. Laurent, teased her mercilessly until she was laughing. He reminded her of the brood of cousins she had at home who all worked for her uncle Gerard's oil business. Those Egerton boys were delightfully wicked when it came to women, but fiercely protective of her like a little sister.

After an hour had passed, she sought refuge from the dancing in an alcove behind the refreshment table. It was a relief to have a moment alone to gather her thoughts. She'd never been overly fond of crowds. She preferred solitude and quiet study whenever possible. Her father said she was like her mother in that way. Rayne's heart ached at the thought. They had lost her two years before, and her death had left her and her father clinging to one another in shared grief.

She was pulled from her thoughts at the rising sound of Adelaide's hateful gossip.

"I don't know why Lady Poole invited those *dreadful* Americans. They're so…" She lowered her voice to say something to her friends that made them laugh. "I mean, look at her dress. It's more suited to a pigsty. Perhaps that's where she grew up? Slopping her way around with the pigs? And her hair —such a lackluster shade of brown. Her face is quite ugly, don't you think? And those eyes—the color of mud."

That was no private conversation of hushed whispers. The woman had wanted her to hear. Had wanted to hurt her. Rayne bit her lip, holding in tears. Adelaide didn't deserve to see her cry. But she felt so helpless and alone. She needed air; she needed quiet.

She rushed toward the nearest door that led out of Lady Poole's ballroom and grabbed the arm of a passing footman in the darkened corridor.

"Please, is there a library here?"

The young man nodded, and he led her to a room a few doors down.

"Is there anything I can get for you, miss?"

"No, thank you. I just need a moment alone." She slipped into the quiet sanctuary and instantly felt more at peace.

A library was the last place anyone would ever come to in the middle of a ball. It was a trick her mother had used when she first debuted in society and needed a moment alone. It was also how her father and mother had met. They had talked for a full evening and missed the entire ball. It had been love at first sight.

Just thinking of that story brought a smile to her lips and calmed her racing heart. She wiped at her eyes, hiding any evidence of her tears that threatened to cling to her lashes. She shouldn't have let Adelaide get to her, but the girl knew just how to hurt someone like her, where her confidence was at its weakest. At least they would only be here a few months. She could stomach that, couldn't she?

For Father's sake, I must.

The library door opened suddenly, and Rayne spun around, heart pounding. She feared Adelaide had followed her here, meaning to finish what she'd started.

CHAPTER 3

A tall, dark-haired man stood framed in the doorway, a dark silhouette against the noise and light from the corridor leading to the ballroom behind him.

He cleared his throat. "My apologies. I thought the room was unoccupied." His voice was pleasant, deep and smooth. It made her think of drinking a glass of brandy and how it made her warm all over. She summoned a polite smile.

"Oh... No, please, I don't mind."

The man hesitated an instant longer before coming inside. As he came into the room, the light from the gas lamps in the corridor outside illuminated him and made her catch her breath. With his intense emerald eyes and handsome face, he looked to be a long-lost prince from some childhood fairy tale her mother used to read. Her eyes moved over his broad shoulders and down to his tapered waist, taking in his tailored but slightly outmoded evening suit just as the strains of a waltz began to play in the distance.

Was this how my mother felt when she first glimpsed my father? A tiny thrill shot through her, like a lightning strike that rippled beneath her skin.

He stared at her for a long moment beneath the hanging oil lamps, and she wondered if it had been a mistake to let him come inside. There was an intensity about him that made her heart race. His green eyes made her think of Zadie, but he was older, perhaps in his thirties, and his features, well... He was striking, if that was the right word to use for a man.

"I could go, if you feel uncomfortable. I just came in here to find a moment of peace," he murmured, his tone all politeness despite the intensity of his green-eyed gaze.

The thought of him leaving, however, left her feeling strangely alone, even though solitude was the reason she had come here. "Please, stay. I suppose it's not at all proper, but..." She didn't finish.

The man chuckled. "I suppose not, but I won't tell a soul if you don't." He took a seat by the fireplace, where flames crackled over logs, and stared into the glowing light.

Rayne waited a moment before joining him. She

carefully arranged her skirts and then sat in a second chair not far from his. Being alone with a strange man like this was exciting, a little frightening too. He made no move toward her, nor engaged her in conversation. He simply gazed at the fire as if the flames held the answers he was seeking. The firelight framed his handsome features, casting a melancholy glow about him that warned her he was deep in his own thoughts. She didn't wish to disturb him, so she took the time to study the clear-cut features of his face. Straight nose, noble chin, and a jaw chiseled from marble. He was possibly one of the most handsome men she had ever met.

"Do you find me interesting?" the man suddenly said.

She jolted a little and blushed at being caught in her secret study of him. "I..." She hesitated but then threw caution to the winds. "Yes, you're very interesting to look at. I'm quite sorry." She laughed a little, the sound slightly nervous. She knew it must be rude to admit such a thing, but this man had a way of drawing truths from her, even though they'd only just met.

The man's half-smile only enhanced his charm. "I suppose that's not a bad thing."

"No, indeed," she assured him.

"You're American?" he asked.

She nodded. Her accent was not what one would

call fully American, but enough to be noticed. Her mother had sent her to a boarding school when she was younger, which gave her a more transatlantic accent. Her mother had hoped it would make her appeal to more gentlemen in the way of obtaining a suitable match.

"No doubt you needed to escape as well," he said. "Balls can either be wonderful or quite dreadful."

"Dreadful was my case."

"The same for me," the man said. "I wanted tonight to be wonderful, but I failed at that quite spectacularly..." His voice trailed off, his focus locked on the fireplace once again. He didn't finish his thought.

"I understand," she replied quietly. "I find myself flustered when I cannot say or do something, and balls seem to be a most limiting place for a woman."

This caught his attention again. He rested an elbow on the arm of the chair and studied her, his chin in his palm.

"And what is it you wished to say or do tonight that you did not?"

"You'll laugh at me," she warned.

"I may. Does that matter?"

Rayne nibbled her bottom lip, wondering how much she ought to say.

"I wanted to pull the curls off a woman's head and wallop her with a fan."

The man burst out laughing. Rather than be embarrassed, she started laughing as well. "Let me guess—Adelaide Berwick has created yet one more enemy?"

"How did you know?" Rayne demanded.

"That creature is the bane of many a ballroom-goer. She can be merciless and gives no quarter to her victims."

"That does seem to be true," Rayne muttered. She still wanted to pull Adelaide's curls off her head.

"Aside from the challenges Lady Adelaide presented, were you enjoying yourself?" For some reason, she flushed with heat. He still watched her with interest. This man didn't know who she was, didn't know about her father's wealth—they were strangers in the candlelight. A whisper of a thrill stole through her, giving her goosebumps on her arms. He noticed her rub at them.

"Cold?" He removed his coat and moved toward her before she could stop him. He draped the black frock coat around her shoulders. She felt oddly shy as the woodsy scent that clung to the dense woolen cheviot cloth made her feel as though he were holding her, not the coat.

"Better?" He took his seat again, and she glanced down at the blend of fabrics, the dark coat against the vulnerable, pale-rose satin of her ball gown. Something about that, the heavy coat atop her, made her shiver again. The man noticed, but he didn't move from his chair again.

"Forget the ball," he said softly. The rich baritone of his voice pulled her focus to him, as though he'd cast some spell over her.

"Forget?"

"Yes. What would you be doing now if you were not here?"

She fisted her skirts nervously. "Now you truly will laugh at me."

"Honestly, tell me. We have the luck of anonymity between us. No one shall know or laugh at what we speak in this sacred realm of books." He raised a hand. "I vow it upon the sanctuary of the library."

Rayne laughed at his solemn expression, and his responding grin stole her breath. She had never seen anything so beautiful before. She saw the delight in his eyes as he looked at her. Aside from her father, she was unaccustomed to being paid attention to as though she mattered. As an heiress, men saw her as a prize to be won, not a woman to be loved.

"If I could be anywhere..." She thought out the answer carefully. "I think I would've liked to have seen the World's Fair at the Crystal Palace that was here earlier this year."

"Oh?" The man's face brightened. "An explorer of the world, are you?"

She grinned back. "Of sciences and the arts, certainly."

"My grandmother and grandfather attended the fair, or the great Exhibition in 1851. It was in Hyde Park then, before it was moved to Sydenham Hill. It was a city of glass and crystal, according to my grandmother."

Rayne leaned forward in her chair, captivated by him. "What did they love best about the fair?"

"My grandfather was taken with the trophy telescope used for viewing the stars."

"The trophy telescope? Why did they call it that?"

"He said it was because the telescope is considered the trophy of the exhibition, but my grandmother had a far more interesting item in mind." The man's eyes twinkled with mischief.

"More interesting than the telescope?" She couldn't imagine what that might be.

"A diamond captured her eye," he answered in a whisper.

"A diamond? How silly." Rayne laughed. She had no interest in gems or jewels. She was practical and valued knowledge above all else.

The man leaned forward a little, as though sharing the world's most important secret. "The diamond was called the Koh-i-noor, which means *mountain of light*. It is one of the world's largest cut diamonds and now rests in the vault of the Tower of

London with the crown jewels. They say it is bad luck to any man who wears it."

"How did the queen acquire it?"

"In the Treaty of Lahore when Britain annexed Punjab in 1849. Ever since, the diamond has courted disaster, and its brilliance has been tainted with blood. Only a female of the royal household is allowed to wear it now." The man continued to speak softly. "My grandmother said it had been bound into an armlet for the queen to wear, with two smaller diamonds flanking it. It rests in a case within black velvet with gas lamps lit around it to make it sparkle. Yet the diamond was flawed and asymmetrical, you see. Prince Albert had it cut for Her Majesty a year after the Great Exhibition, but my grandmother said that day when she saw it, she looked at it head-on, and the uncut gem drew her in like a black cavernous hole, and she said..." The man paused.

"Said what?" Rayne was hanging upon his every word. "Tell me, *please*." She scooted her chair closer to his, until their knees touched.

The man still stared at her, his gaze fathomless as he continued. "She claimed that the diamond showed her half a millennium of bloodshed. Every man who'd held the diamond bore its curse and died. Then my grandmother saw it resting in a crown."

"But is it in the crown now?"

The man shook his head. "No, not yet. It is still in

a bracelet that belongs to the queen. I've seen it myself. But I believe my grandmother saw the future."

Rayne gasped. "You've seen it?" Unthinkingly, she reached out to touch his hand on the armrest close to hers.

"Yes. The queen rarely wears the Koh-i-noor. She claims it makes her uneasy, but she still wears it to some state functions. I glimpsed it upon her wrist a few years ago." His gaze grew distant as he seemed to recall the memory. "The way the light glinted off it... I felt like a sailor lured to the rocks by a siren's call. Then I blinked, and the desire to possess it was gone. I felt as though I'd woken from a dark and terrible nightmare."

Rayne's lips parted in shock at the man's fantastic tale, wanting to believe he was teasing her, but she heard the truth in his voice.

"I wish I could've seen it. Not because I like pretty baubles. I do not, but..."

He chuckled. "You have no need of jewels. The beauty of your eyes and the brilliance of your mind are far more attractive than a diamond about your neck."

His frank words startled her. "You think I'm pretty?" Her face flushed, and a happiness blossomed within her in a way that had never happened before when a man praised her looks. Those men had only sought her money, but this man? He had no designs up on her fortune; he was simply looking at her. Longing stirred within her, and she knew for the first time in her life how a lady might easily be compromised by the right man in the right moment...a moment such as this.

"No, not at all," he said flatly. The blossoming hope inside her began to wither. She dropped her gaze, hoping to hide her dismay from him, but he lifted her chin with a finger. "I think you are *stunning*." That rich voice sent wild shivers through her. "*Pretty* is a word for young girls with bows in their hair. *You* are exquisite."

He reached up to trace her gently winged brows and the slightly upward curve of her nose, then slipped his fingers over her cheekbones and down to her chin before resting on her lips. He brushed the pad of his thumb over her mouth, and a dark hunger she'd never experienced before stirred to life. She reacted without thinking, pressing her lips to his thumb and then flicking her tongue against it.

He froze and inhaled sharply. Their eyes locked. Rayne's stomach started to tumble inside her as she feared she'd let her newfound desire take her too far.

"May I steal a kiss, sweet stranger of mine?" the man asked, his low, hypnotic voice irresistible.

"I've never been kissed before," she admitted. And at that moment she wanted him to be the first.

She wanted it more than she'd wanted anything in her entire life.

Her heart stuttered as his eyes darkened with desire. A devilish smile covered his face. There was a possessive look to it, one that said once he began to kiss her, she would beg him never to stop because she would be forever under his spell.

He lifted her easily from the chair and into his lap. Rayne grasped his shoulders, feeling the heat of his body pour into hers. She couldn't resist leaning closer to him.

The man cupped the back of her head, and she leaned into him. They both paused an inch apart, and she savored that building anticipation until his lips touched hers. Her stomach swirled as his warm mouth gently explored hers. It was a kiss of seduction in tender measure. The delicious sensation of their mouths moving together made her blood sing and her head light. Her corset tightened almost painfully as she struggled for breath. She drank in the sweetness of his taste, and a deep-seated need coiled low in her abdomen as he licked at the seam of her lips. She parted her mouth and gasped in shock as his tongue found hers.

The dreamlike intimacy set her heart to trembling anew. Her mind drifted deeper into his kiss. She imagined them seated just like this, her on his lap, a Christmas tree behind them and a kissing bough above them. The man in her dream looked up at her, and in his eyes she saw a future, a life she had never dreamed of before. A potent longing, so intense, made her stiffen in his arms, but she didn't pull away. A sudden fear of losing all this was almost overpowering.

The man held her tight, his kiss intensifying, and Rayne surrendered to the delicious, dark mastery he now held over her body. The fiery possession of his lips sent excitement like she'd never experienced before rippling through her. Her blood pounded, and her knees trembled. She was grateful to be on his lap, clinging to him with everything she had. His hands moved down her body, the heat of his palms seeping through the layers of cloth. A dozen emotions she could barely register whirled around her head as their lips finally, reluctantly separated.

The man was breathing as hard as she was. They both smiled a little shyly as they looked at each other. His eyes roamed over her face, and there was a softness to his expression that made her heart flip in her chest.

"Thank you," he whispered as he grazed the back of his hand against her cheek.

"For what?" Rayne asked.

He was silent a bit longer before he replied. "For showing me what it could have been like."

Confused, she waited for an explanation, but

none was forthcoming. The large grandfather clock in the corner struck the late hour.

"We should go before we're missed," he said.

Rayne slipped off his lap, her head a little muddled still from the stranger's drugging kiss. She couldn't find any words as she reluctantly removed his coat from her body and held it out to him. Their hands met as he accepted the woolen frock coat.

"I wish...," the man began, then gave a rueful shake of his head.

"Please... What do you wish?" She had to resist the urge to reach out and touch him again.

"I wish we could have met under different circumstances." The man cupped her chin and leaned down, feathering his lips over hers with one last ghost of a kiss. Then he brushed a finger along her bodice, and she gasped as he plucked a fresh rose from her décolletage and held it up to his nose, breathing in the scent.

"A token. To remember you," he said with a melancholy smile. Then, before she could stop him, he was gone.

Rayne stared at the open doorway, her heart racing with joy and yet strangely painful. Could she fall in love with a stranger and have her heart broken at the same time? There had been some magic at work, something that had drawn them together, and it left her feeling desolate now that he had gone.

She clutched her skirts and tried to calm herself. She waited a few minutes before returning to the ball. Everything around her seemed the same, yet she had changed. Some great change had indeed begun inside her, something that could not be undone, nor did she wish it to be erased.

If only...

❦

OLIVER HELD THE ROSE BLOOM IN HIS PALM AS HE met his family on the stairs outside Lady Poole's home. The scent returned him to that memory of the mysterious woman in the library. He would have given anything to drop to one knee and ask her, whoever she was, to be his wife instead of Adelaide. He'd tasted desire on the woman's lips, had glimpsed her keen mind, and had seen a future with her as they'd talked. A future that could not be. Regret clawed a hollow space within his heart as he knew he would never see her again, nor ever know who she was.

He barely listened to his family's chattering as they waited for a hackney to take them to Grosvenor Square. They piled in after one came to a stop, and Everett jostled him with an elbow as he sat down beside Oliver.

"Well, how did it go?"

"Pardon?" Oliver was still replaying that lingering, too perfect kiss. He didn't even know her name, and that was all the better because tonight was all that they could ever have, an exquisite, life-altering kiss.

"What about Adelaide? Did you propose?"

Oliver cradled the rose in his hands as he looked up at the faces of his family. Guilt stabbed at his gut as he realized he'd failed them.

"I didn't. We spoke briefly, and I had every intention of asking her, but…"

"But…?" Everett prompted.

"I needed a minute to clear my head." *And then I met the most enchanting mystery woman in the library.* "And by the time I got back, she'd left."

That woman had changed everything for him. He had found a kindred spirit in her. The connection between them had been intense. He had spoken of cursed diamonds and old memories and lost himself in her eyes.

"Oliver." His mother spoke his name softly, but the concern in her tone caught his attention, pulling it away from the thoughts of the American girl in the pale-pink gown covered with real, blossoming roses.

"Are you holding a rose?" Zadie suddenly asked.

He glanced at his sister and nodded, still clutching the velvet-soft petals of the precious bloom. He had been unable to resist claiming the rose that had featured so prominently above such beautiful breasts. Her breath had quickened as he'd removed the rose from her gown. His desire—yes, desire, not simple lust—had been excruciating, but he had found the courage to walk away as the clock struck midnight, if only because he'd claimed this token of her. Zadie would've teased him for being caught up in a fairy tale or some other nonsense, but the magic in that room had been real. He wouldn't deny it.

"Where did you get it?" Zadie asked, her eyes still focused on the rose.

"I...," he stammered.

"Oliver... Did you take it from Miss Egerton?" There was a strange note of hope in Zadie's voice.

"What? Who?"

"Miss Rayne Egerton, the American. She was at the ball with her father tonight. She wore the most beautiful pale-rose gown with real roses sewn into it." Zadie pointed at the bloom in his palm. "Like that one."

"But what about Adelaide?" their mother interrupted. "Shouldn't we focus on how Oliver will find a chance to offer for her?"

Zadie ignored their mother as stared at Oliver with a calculating look that bothered him. "You did meet her? Rayne, I mean?"

"We never introduced ourselves. We talked and..." He did not want to admit he'd kissed her as though he might not live to see the dawn in front of his sister and mother.

"Oliver," Zadie said, "Rayne is an *heiress*—far richer than Adelaide."

The occupants of the coach were silent as Zadie's words sank in.

"You mean..." Everett began to chuckle in delight. "We have someone else to choose from besides old Adelaide? Thank Christ!"

"Everett," Margaret admonished, then turned to Oliver. "Is it true? You met the American heiress tonight? Is she lovely?"

"The loveliest," he assured her, though he was still in shock. His beautiful stranger was an heiress and could be the solution to saving his family and his home. Surely life couldn't be that kind to bless him that way. He buried the sudden guilt at the thought that she might come to hate him if she ever learned how desperate he was to marry her. With Adelaide, she would have known about his situation and understood. Matches for wealth were common, but Rayne? She didn't come from a country that had titles or placed much value on them. He could only hope she'd believe his interest in her was genuine and that he wanted to marry her for more than just her money.

Margaret sighed. "How would we even find her again? These Americans always come and go on a whim, and we are due to leave for Lord Fraser's in a few days."

Zadie beamed in excitement and nudged Oliver. "She will be in attendance at Lord Fraser's house party too. She's taking a train tomorrow afternoon, and I think you should be on it."

"What?" Oliver asked. "My ticket is for three days hence with you."

Zadie shook her head. "No, you need to be alone, and you need to woo her on the train before she arrives at Lord Fraser's. We don't want Adelaide ruining your fortune hunting."

Oliver grimaced at the term. *Fortune hunting.* He didn't want to think of Rayne like that, yet trapping her in a tiny cabin aboard a train to steal a dozen more kisses... That was the sort of hunt he wouldn't mind at all, as long as he could ignore the creeping feeling of guilt about luring Rayne into marriage.

"Do you like her, Oliver?" his mother asked. "Only pursue her if you do. At least with Adelaide we know the kind of person we're dealing with."

His little brother snorted and winked at Oliver. "*Anyone* is better than Adelaide."

"Everett!" Margaret hushed him.

Oliver smiled, feeling hopeful for the first time as he looked at his mother and siblings. "I do. I like her very much."

Now all he had to do was seduce an heiress on a

train in two days to save his family and his home. How hard could it be?

WANT TO KNOW WHAT HAPPENS NEXT? GRAB IT wherever ebooks are sold or listen to it as part of the 2 book audiobook collection called Dashing Through the Snow found wherever audiobooks are sold!

Visit www.laurensmithbooks.com to find this and other passionate romances by Lauren Smith!

Lauren Smith is an Oklahoma attorney by day, author by night who pens adventurous and edgy romance stories by the light of her smart phone flashlight app. She knew she was destined to be a romance writer when she attempted to re-write the entire *Titanic* movie just to save Jack from drowning. Connecting with readers by writing emotionally moving, realistic and sexy romances no matter what time period is her passion. She's won multiple awards in several romance subgenres including: New England Reader's Choice Awards, Greater Detroit BookSeller's Best Awards, and a Semi-Finalist award for the Mary Wollstonecraft Shelley Award.

To connect with Lauren visit her at:
www.laurensmithbooks.com
lauren@laurensmithbooks.com

facebook.com/LaurenDianaSmith

twitter.com/LSmithAuthor

bookbub.com/authors/lauren-smith

OTHER TITLES BY LAUREN
SMITH

Historical
The League of Rogues Series
Wicked Designs

His Wicked Seduction

Her Wicked Proposal

Wicked Rivals

Her Wicked Longing

His Wicked Embrace

The Earl of Pembroke

His Wicked Secret

The Last Wicked Rogue

Never Kiss a Scot

The Earl of Kent

Never Tempt a Scot

The Seduction Series
The Duelist's Seduction

The Rakehell's Seduction
The Rogue's Seduction
The Gentleman's Seduction
Standalone Stories
Tempted by A Rogue
Bewitching the Earl
Bewitching an Heiress on a Train
Sins and Scandals
An Earl By Any Other Name
A Gentleman Never Surrenders
A Scottish Lord for Christmas

Contemporary
Ever After Series
Legally Charming
The Surrender Series
The Gilded Cuff
The Gilded Cage
The Gilded Chain
The Darkest Hour
Love in London
Forbidden
Seduction
Climax
Forever Be Mine

Paranormal
Dark Seductions Series

The Shadows of Stormclyffe Hall
The Love Bites Series
The Bite of Winter
His Little Vixen
Brotherhood of the Blood Moon Series
Blood Moon on the Rise (coming soon)
Brothers of Ash and Fire
Grigori: A Royal Dragon Romance
Mikhail: A Royal Dragon Romance
Rurik: A Royal Dragon Romance

Sci-Fi Romance
Cyborg Genesis Series
Across the Stars

The Krinar Eclipse
The Krinar Code by Emma Castle